Violet and The Connect 2

Tina J

Copyright 2019

Warning:

This book is strictly Urban Fiction and the story is **NOT**

REAL!

Characters will not behave the way you want them to; nor will

they react to situations the way you think they should. Some of

them may be drug addicts, kingpins, savages, thugs, rich, poor,

ho's, sluts, haters, bitter ex-girlfriends or boyfriends, people

from the past and the list can go on and on. That is what Urban

Fiction mostly consists of. If this isn't anything you foresee

yourself interested in, then do yourself a favor and don't read it

because it's only going to piss you off. □□

Also, the book will not end the way you want so please be

advised that the outcome will be based solely on my own

thoughts and ideas. I hope you enjoy this book that y'all made

me write. Thanks so much to my readers, supporters, publisher

and fellow authors and authoress for the support. □□

Author Tina J

More books from me:

The Thug I Chose 1, 2 & 3

A Thin Line Between Me and My Thug 1 & 2

I Got Luv For My Shawty 1 & 2

Kharis and Caleb: A Different Kind of Love 1 & 2

Loving You Is A Battle 1 & 2 & 3

Violet and The Connect 1 & 2 & 3

You Complete Me

Love Will Lead You Back

This Thing Called Love

Are We In This Together 1,2 &3

Shawty Down To Ride For a Boss 1, 2 &3

When A Boss Falls in Love 1, 2 & 3

Let Me Be The One 1 & 2

We Got That Forever Love

Aint No Savage Like The One I Got 1&2

A Queen and A Hustla 1, 2 & 3

Thirsty For A Bad Boy 1&2

Hassan and Serena: An Unforgettable Love 1&2

My Brother's Keeper 1. 2 & 3

C'Yani & Meek: A Dangerous Hood Love 1, 2 & 3

When A Savage Falls for A Good Girl 1, 2 & 3

Eva & Deray 1 & 2

Blame It On His Gangsta Luv 1 & 2

Falling For The Wrong Hustla 1, 2 & 3

I Gave My Heart To A Jersey Killa 1, 2 & 3

<u>Violet</u>

Heaven picked me up from the airport and dropped me off at my mom's house. My ex Dom was released a few years early from prison and his boys were throwing him a party. I can't believe twenty years had gone by. I wasn't going to go at first, but the girls talked me into it.

I threw on a white strapless Rebecca Strapless Sequined Cocktail Dress from BCBG that fit my body like a glove; with some nude pumps. I pulled my hair up in a ponytail and wore my diamond studs. I never wore a lot of makeup but my lip-gloss stayed popping. Mariah picked me up and Ang and Heaven were behind us in another car.

The guys were already at the club when we got there. Heaven sent Dayquan a text and he came outside to get us. As usual it was way too many people in one spot. The guys were up in VIP so the girls and me decided to dance. *Say it* by Tory

Lanez was playing. I didn't see Dom anywhere, but I knew he would find me and he did.

"You are still beautiful." He whispered in my ear as he danced behind me.

After the song went off, I turned around and gave him a hug. He was still sexy as hell. He wore Gucci everything, his hair was freshly cut and the waves were drowning me. His smile always got to me.

"And you look good Dom. How long have you been home?" He and I got reacquainted like he never left.

I saw all the chicks staring; one in particular who I'm sure was the one who would be occupying his time. We exchanged numbers and he returned to VIP. I felt his gaze on me the entire night and that was fine because I was doing the same thing.

My phone started vibrating and it was Miguel calling. I ignored the call because if it was an emergency Hazel would've called me.

"So you're going to just ignore my calls?" I felt his breath on the back of my neck and my panties became soaked.

I missed him so much. I turned around and I felt like I was about to have an orgasm off his looks alone. I can't even describe what he had on because I was drooling myself. I saw all the chicks pointing and trying to find out who he was.

"You like what you see Violet?" I took a sip of my drink and tried to get off the seat.

"What do you want Miguel? Is Jr. ok?" He took my hand and led me to the dance floor. I saw my girls staring and laughing.

"This what happen when I think about you, I get in my feelings yo, I start reminiscing yo, next time around, fuck I want it to be different yo, waiting on a sign, guess its time for a different prayer, Lord please save her for me, Do this one favor for me, I had to change my player ways, it got way too complicated for me, I hope she's waiting for me."

We were grinding on each other to Bryson Tiller's song *Exchange*. He was singing the song in my ear and I wanted to fuck him right there. The hardness from his dick was rubbing against my ass.

"I miss you V." The hairs on the back of my neck were standing up.

"Miguel don't do this."

"Don't do what? I'm just dancing." He pushed my hair on one side and sucked on my neck. He turned me around and stuck his tongue in my mouth.

"Yo, why every time you two get together y'all look like you're about to fuck on the dance floor?" Dayquan was talking shit as usual. I put my head down laughing.

"I see you came for your woman huh?" He asked Miguel.

"Yea, something like that."

"Well V. I guess you're calling it a night." Heaven said.

"I didn't plan on leaving yet." Miguel lifted my ass up right off the dance floor and walked me out the club.

"Call me later." Heaven yelled and stayed on the dance floor with her husband.

"Hey Ms. V. It's been a long time." Carlos said.

"I know. How are you? And how's my girl Keisha?"
She was his wife. She and I were cool but I haven't really
spoken to anyone since I left Miguel.

"She's good. She told me to tell you y'all still having a
girl's night out." He and I conversed a little longer until the
truck stopped at the Waldorf Astoria hotel. He rented the
penthouse on the 42nd floor. The room was fucking beautiful.

"What are we doing here Miguel?"

"I want to talk to you and since you're missing, this
was the only way I could get to you."

"Fine. Talk." He got on his knees in front of me and
spread my legs open.

"This isn't talking Miguel." I tried to close my legs, but
he was too strong.

"Yo, you came outside with no panties on?"

"Miguel, you can't wear them with this dress."

"Then you shouldn't have worn the dress."

"What are you mad for? I'm single remember." I gave
him a phony smile.

"Violet, the first time I stuck my dick in you, you became mine. It doesn't matter what goes on with us, this pussy belongs to me." I couldn't even respond because his mouth covered my pearl; which erupted as soon as he touched her.

"Mmmmm she still tastes sweet as ever. You know what I want V. Are you going to give it to me?" He always wanted me to experience a big O with him. He claims it showed him how much I really enjoyed it.

He was right though; I never had so many of them; let alone him leaving me with the feeling like my juices gush out like a waterfall. He had my body experiencing so many things I couldn't see myself with anyone else.

"Take it from me. Fuck. Miguel make me cum baby." He pulled at least four more out. The chair I was sitting in was soaked with my juices. I stood up and removed my dress.

"Where did this scar come from?" He ran his fingers above my pussy to feel it.

"Never mind that."

"Nah V. What happened to you?" I saw the concern in his eyes. I couldn't give him the answer he was looking for without hurting him. I wasn't ready to talk about it. I slid down on his dick slowly and screamed out. I hadn't had sex with anyone since him so I was virgin tight once again for him.

"Shit baby. I see you kept her tight for me."

"Miguel, I love you so much. Why did you hurt me?" He wiped the tears from my face and covered my mouth with his. I rode him until we both climaxed.

"I love you too V and I don't know why I keep fucking up. I need you in my life but I can't have you right now." He said sucking on my chest.

"I keep hurting you. I hate seeing you cry and you're the mother of my son and was supposed to be my wife. I know you don't think it's affecting me, but it is. When you hurt I do too."

"Then why can't you get it together for us?"

"V. I'm in no position to be tied down right now. I know it's selfish of me but I want you to wait for me."

"You mean wait for you to finish fucking around." I started putting my clothes on. I was fuming and he knew it.

"Violet you and my son are everything to me. I'm lost without you but I don't wanna bring you back in my life full time and constantly bring you pain."

"Well then let me go Miguel."

"HELL NO!!!!!!"

"Miguel, I can't do this anymore. I waited months for you to come get me and when you do, you still want me to wait. I don't understand you."

"What do you want from me V?" He was sitting on the chair staring at me with his arms on his legs.

"Just you. I don't want anything but you, your heart, your love."

"V, you have all that. No one else can get any of that."

"No, but they can get your body." He put his head down.

"Goodbye Miguel."

"V, you're not leaving."

"Yes, I am." He snatched my arm and held me close.

"No you're not. I'm not letting you walk out of my life again for months at a time and then I can't find you."

"I won't do that. Now that I know how you feel I will send you my address to come visit the kids. All I ask is that you don't let that woman around them."

"Kids. V we only have a son." At that moment, the tears clouded my vision and I ran out the room. I could hear him screaming my name down the hall as the elevator came.

"V. Stop this running shit. What the fuck is going on?"

"I'm sorry Miguel." I stepped on the elevator and he came in behind me.

"Talk to me V. What are you sorry about?" When the elevator finally opened on the ground floor we stepped out.

"V STOP!" I put my hand up for a cab.

"What?"

"Talk to me. What kids?" A cab pulled up and I went to step on the curb. I saw Miguel standing there waiting for me to answer. I went to speak when I saw a huge truck coming full speed towards me.

"VIOLET MOVEEEEE!!!!!" I heard Miguel scream

before everything went black.

Miguel

I watched Violet's body get tossed in the air like a basketball. The truck was aiming straight for her, there was no doubt about it. The cab broke her fall from hitting the ground. I ran over to her and she had blood dripping from her head and mouth, a bone popped through the skin in her arm, I couldn't tell where the other injuries were from because blood saturated her white dress. I put her head on top of my lap and moved the hair out of her face.

"Oh my God. Somebody call the ambulance." I heard people yelling behind me.

"Baby wake up." I waited for her to open her eyes but she didn't. I felt the tears running down my face.

It didn't matter how many people I murdered I had no remorse, but the way Violet's lifeless body laid in my arms had my emotions on 100.

"Boss, come on. The ambulance is here. Let them take her." Carlos said bringing me out of my thoughts. I didn't wanna let her go but I needed to.

"Where's the truck?" Carlos told me it left right after it hit her but we got the license plate number. I jumped in the car and started making phone calls. The first one was to her sister. I knew everyone was still out and together.

"Hey brother in law, did my sister kick you out already?" I just laughed because she knew we were going through some issues.

"Mariah, there was an accident." I told her.

"WHAT? Is my sister ok?"

"Mariah, you need to get to the hospital." Carlos had to follow the ambulance because we had no idea where the hospital was.

"The hospital. What the fuck is going on?" Mitch took the phone from her and I explained as much as possible without breaking down myself.

Once we got there, I sent Mitch a text of where it was. I then sent one to Ricardo telling him the jet was on its way back to get him, my mom and my son. If my sister wanted to come, she could but right now I wasn't feeling her either.

I jumped out when we got there and followed the EMT's inside. They took her to the back and started working on her immediately. You could hear doctors being paged, along with x-ray technicians, nurses and so forth.

One of the nurses came over to have me fill out information on her. Mariah took the paperwork out my hand and filled it out herself because my hands weren't moving. I hadn't even noticed them come in. The guys gave me a hug and we all sat down in the waiting room for the doctor.

It was about six in the morning and we still hadn't heard anything from the doctors. They sent the nurses out every hour to tell us they'll be out soon to talk to us. My mom, sister, Ricardo, my niece and son arrived. They were wide-awake and started terrorizing shit the minute they got here.

"What happened? Is she going to be ok?" My mom asked.

"The cab was hit from behind which caused the truck to hit parked cars in the process. Because she was about to get in, her body was tossed in the air and landed on the cab. She's been back there for a long time." My mom hugged me. The doctor walked out as I let her go.

"Are you the family of Violet Rodriguez?" I looked at Mariah and she smirked. I told Violet I changed her name but I wasn't sure if she told anyone, but I guess she did.

"Yes."

"Ok, let's have a seat over here." There was no one in the waiting room, which is why he didn't take us in the back.

"Violet is going to be fine." I let out a huge sigh and so did everyone else.

"She has a broken collar bone which caused a compound fracture. What you saw Mr.?" He waited for me to answer.

"Rodriguez."

"Oh you're the husband?" He asked.

"Something like that."

"Ok, because she was asking for you." I smiled when he said that.

"Her bone popped out the skin, so we had to repair it in surgery which is why it took us so long to come speak to you.

She also has a concussion, some cracked ribs and one of her legs had some swelling in it. When we checked she had a blood clot in there, so we took care of that as well. She will be in an extreme amount of pain for a while. I'm sending her home with a morphine drip that will dispense every few hours to keep her comfortable."

"When can she go home?" I asked.

"I'm going to keep her for another day or two just to make sure she's ok. If everything looks good, she can leave Monday or Tuesday." He stood up and shook our hands.

"They have her room ready if you guys want to wait in there for her to come out of recovery. Mr. Rodriguez can I speak to you in private?" I wasn't sure what he wanted to speak about.

"What's up doc?"

"Mrs. Rodriguez was asking for you after they brought her in and kept repeating something about not telling you about joy. I have no idea what that means; maybe you know." I shook my head and thanked the doctor. One of the nurses came out and escorted us up to the room V was going to be in.

"I know it's a lot of you here and I'm sorry about what happened to your loved one. I just need you guys to keep it down for our other patients." We all nodded our heads at her.

I told Mariah what the doctor said and it seemed that the room got quiet. I was about to speak when the door opened, and they brought Violet in on a stretcher. Her face lit up when she saw me. Well I'm assuming it was for me because she didn't see anyone else yet. I was closest to the door.

The nurses locked the wheels on the stretcher, checked her vitals and stepped out. Jr. wanted to sit on the bed with her, but she was in too much pain. I let him kiss her and gave him back to my mom.

There was a knock at the door and it was Violet's mom and dad. They were carrying a car set covered with a pink blanket. Her dad passed me the car seat and I had no idea why. They ran over to V kissing her face and saying prayers for her.

"Miguel." I heard Violet trying to call my name. I was removing the blanket from the car seat. It was hot in the hospital and didn't want the baby to burn up.

"MIGUEL!!!!" She was trying to yell out. I took the blanket off without looking and stepped over to V.

"Yea baby." She had so many tears running down her face.

"Why you crying so hard Violet?" The room was silent; you could hear a pin drop.

"I'm sorry." She was crying hysterical.

"Sorry for what?" I wiped her eyes and felt someone tap me on my shoulder. I turned around and Heaven placed a tiny replica of Jr. in my hands. This baby couldn't have been more than two months old.

"Heaven whose baby is this?" in my heart I felt she was mine, but I needed for someone to tell me that.

"Miguel. This is Joy Alexis." Then it dawned on me. Before the accident she kept saying kids and then the doctor said, she didn't want me to know about Joy. I know V didn't have my daughter and didn't tell me.

"Violet tell me right now. Is this my daughter?" I wanted her to look me in the face and tell me.

"Miguel."

"No V. IS THIS MY DAUGHTER?" I said it through gritted teeth because I didn't want to yell. She put her head down.

"Yes." She tried to whisper.

"I can't hear you."

"Yes Miguel. That's your daughter."

"Nah, this can't be my daughter because you would never do me like that. I know we were going through some shit but there's no way you wouldn't tell me I had another kid." When she didn't say anything, I gave the baby back to Heaven.

"I'm gone." I kissed my son and walked out.

"Miguel." I heard her tryna yell for me but my pride wouldn't let me turn around.

Violet

I remember Miguel asking me what I meant when I said kids, a truck coming and then everything went black. I'm not sure if it was an accident or done on purpose but I'm sure Miguel will find out and handle it.

When they brought me to my room, I was happy to see him standing there waiting for me. I knew I had to hurt him when my parents walked in with Joy. I never got the chance to tell him and even though I should've never held that secret, I saw the hurt and pain written on his face when he found out.

I found out I was pregnant the day I walked out on him. I thought he knew and didn't care because when I threw the results at him it was on the paperwork. I'm not saying it was his responsibility to look over the results, but I figured he would. I didn't find out I was pregnant until I was already four months and Jr. was five months. I got pregnant the same day the doctor gave the damn green light to have sex again. I still had regular periods; they were light, but a period is a period if you ask me.

Anyway, I had a burning feeling in my stomach, and I knew he was cheating so that only meant one thing. I didn't expect to hear I had Chlamydia too. I was hurt, embarrassed and felt like he didn't deserve to know about my baby. The moment she told me I was pregnant after the pee test, I planned on terminating it until she needed to do an ultrasound to see how far along I was.

I think the doctor did the shit on purpose. She knew I didn't want it. I feel like she turned the machine up loud and turned the screen just enough so I could see it. Once she did, it was a wrap as far as termination. She saw the smile on my face and she in return did the same.

"Do you want to know what you're having?" I looked at her crazy.

"Can you tell? I thought it was too early."

"We usually like to wait until you are in your fifth month to be sure but the baby is showing everything right now."

"Sure. Why not?"

"It's a girl." The tears cascaded down my face like rain. The doctor tried to console me. I missed Miguel so much and he should've been here with me to enjoy it with me.

I got dressed, got my pre natal vitamins and left. I made up my mind to stay with him and try to fix what was broken in our relationship. All that changed when he came home running to the shower. Just watching him and knowing another woman received the pleasure he gave me, pissed me off. The fact he gave me not one but two diseases, I changed my mind.

I stayed in a hotel for a few days under Hazel's name and moved into a house she had built for her and Ricardo two and a half hours from him. I wasn't going back to the states. Jr. needed his father and I know his dad needed him too.

After about a week I broke down and called Miguel on his cell. His ex answered the phone and told me he was in the shower. I don't know about all women, but I know when you're still in love with a man and another chic answers and says he's in the shower, it's like a shot in the heart and not by cupid.

I thought about his body dripping wet and how he probably sexed her in there. All the things we did in the shower and how he was doing them with her. I was driving myself crazy thinking about what he was doing with another woman and he didn't give two shits about me. How stupid was I? I finally made the decision to keep Joy a secret. Hazel only found out because she came over every weekend. The day I gave birth, I almost died.

It was a Friday afternoon and the nanny had taken Jr. out for a walk. Hazel walked in just as I started cramping and within minutes, my water broke. She told me my body shut down and I started having a seizure. When the EMT got me to the hospital I started hemorrhaging and the umbilical cord was wrapped around my baby's neck. I always told Hazel to record the birth so I could show Miguel when we were on better terms.

The night I gave birth, Hazel took Jr. to his moms' house and he was staying for two weeks. I felt it was time to tell Miguel but again when I called his office phone me and his bitch got into it. I was done for good after that. If he allowed her to answer his phones, he had to know what she was doing and saying. I felt disrespected and humiliated and he didn't deserve to know about Joy.

Now here I am sitting in a hospital because I almost died trying to tell him he had another baby. He stormed out of here with Carlos and Joe behind him, followed by my brothers. I know they would talk to him but the hurt I saw in his eyes was enough to make me feel like shit.

"Fuck that. I'm not going to feel bad for him anymore. If he didn't cheat on me with that bitch we wouldn't even be in this situation."

"VIOLET!" My mother yelled out.

"Yes ma."

"Don't you dare sit there and put the blame on him. Yes, he messed up sleeping with the other woman, but it was your responsibility to make sure he knew about Joy. You're lucky I was unaware you didn't tell him because I would have."

"Violet, I'm very disappointed in you." My father said shaking his head. He was in the corner with Jr. on his lap.

"Who else knew about the baby?" Miguel's mom asked.

"We found out when she came yesterday." Ang spoke up.

"Hazel." Neither she nor I would look at one another.

"HAZEL!!!!!!" Her mom screamed at her. She started tearing up and Ricardo walked out pissed off.

"Oh my God Hazel. Miguel is going to kill you. How could you?"

"Ma please. I know and don't think I didn't tell Violet over and over she needed to tell him."

"Violet, you and Hazel are dead wrong. Whatever my son did to you, he didn't deserve this."

"I know. Can everybody just go please? I'm tired and need some time to myself." I gave my babies a kiss and said goodbye to everyone. I really was in a lot of pain. I tried to sleep but I had this eerie feeling that someone was in the room with me. I pressed the nurse's button.

"Are you ok Mrs. Rodriguez?" She asked coming closer to where I was.

"Yes. Has anyone been in this room?"

"No. Besides everyone who left, no one has been in here. I came in to take your vitals not too long ago and you were asleep."

"Ok. Thanks."

"Are you ok?"

"Yes. I'm fine." She walked out. I wasn't about to tell her what I was feeling and then some psychiatrist come in telling me I'm seeing or hearing shit. I was not going to be locked up with a straight jacket. I laid in the darkness trying to decide if I should text Miguel and as much as my mind said no, my heart said yes.

Me: *Miguel, I'm so sorry you found out about your daughter Joy this way. There were so many times I reached out to tell you and something always came up. I want to sit down and talk to you about why I made the decision not to. If you don't want to, I understand. Here's my address to my new place and Hazel is going to keep the kids for a week or two so I can rest.*

I hit send and put my phone on the tray table thing in front of me. I was released from the hospital two days later and instead of taking the jet like his mom asked, I flew commercial. I was still in my feelings of him not texting me back, so I didn't want to use shit from him. Hazel picked me up from the airport since she was back before me.

"You know my mom cursed me out the entire night over you and my niece?"

"I know Hazel. I'm sorry I got you involved. I should've told him but whenever I got the courage up to tell him, she stood in the way."

"Fuck her. She's just jealous you came and took him from her."

"I wouldn't say that."

"You did. She's been with my brother for so many years and she ran everyone off. He didn't care either because he would just find a new bitch; however, you stole his heart, love and mind. Her ass is going crazy trying to figure out how you did it that quick."

We pulled up to my house and I got the same eerie feeling I had in the hospital like I was being watched. I told Hazel but she said I was being paranoid, and no one knew where I was.

"I reached out to your brother the night he found out about Joy and I haven't heard from him since."

"That's weird." She said driving.

"Why you say that?"

"Because he told my mom the least you could've done was tried to call and explain yourself." We looked at each other and shook our heads. The only person we could think of was Faith.

"She probably deleted the message before he saw it." Hazel said helping me out the car.

"You haven't spoke to him." When she told me no I knew something must've happened. They talked quite a few times a day. She told me the shit hit the fan at Jr. party with her and Faith and how she let him know my ex was checking for me. I wasn't worried because even though Dom was looking good as hell; Miguel was still the only one on my mind.

Hazel opened the door but stopped me before I could go in. She glanced at the two trucks that had two bodyguards each in them and nodded her head. She backed me down the steps and before I could ask what was going on, gunfire erupted throughout the house.

One of the bodyguards grabbed me and had me sit down in Hazel's car which was bulletproof. Ever since the shit happened with the Africans every car was made this way. If you asked me, they should've always been but Miguel felt like he wasn't beefing that hard with anyone. She got back in the car, backed out quickly and started driving like a bat out of hell.

"I'm taking you to my mom's house."

"Ok. Did you see who it was?"

"Yes." She answered but said nothing else.

"Then why are we leaving? They should be dead."

"The house is gone V."

"What do you mean gone?"

"I mean you don't live there anymore. It had to be burned. I'm sorry; you can stay with me, my mom or him." She pointed to her brother who was pulling away from the house. Thank goodness he didn't see us. I was not in the mood.

I went inside and laid down in one of the bedrooms. This was a long ass day and I was over it.

Hazel

Violet told me she had a feeling someone was watching her at the hospital, but to get her home and find out niggas were in her house trying to kill her, was another story.

At first, I didn't know who it was because Miguel got rid of the Africans and the new guy who took over, was cool with us. There was no one who came to mind until I saw the faces when we removed their masks.

It was Reggie who used to work for my brother along with some other guys. I know he was mad at him but why would he take it out on V when he didn't know her? Something wasn't adding up, but I knew when Miguel found out there was a hit out on his baby mother, he was going to lose it. What if she had the kids with her?

"Where is she?" He yelled into my phone when I answered it.

"Oh, you're talking to me." I sarcastically said.

"Cut the shit. Where is she?"

"Lying down in mommy's room." I looked over the couch and the door was closed.

"How is she? Was she hit?" I could hear the concern.

"No she's fine. It didn't really faze her."

"Why do you say that?"

"She told me earlier she felt like someone was watching her in the hospital, but she nixed it off. I'm started to think maybe it was."

"Why didn't you tell me?"

"She just told me today."

"Yea ok. I'll be by later to see my kids." I don't think he believed me but it was the truth.

"Oh you're acknowledging Joy?"

"Hazel don't fucking start. She went all this time without uttering a single word to me about being pregnant and I'm supposed to be excited when a baby is put in my arms?"

"I didn't say that."

"Exactly. No matter which way you look at it, she was foul. She could've told me. FUCK!!!!" I could tell he was getting pissed just talking about it.

"Miguel, she tried to tell you but once again that bitch kept getting in the way." I tried to make sense of why Violet kept it away.

"What bitch?"

"Come on Mickey. You know who I'm talking about."

"Whatever. V knew how to find me; I just couldn't find her."

"Mickey, I think you should really listen to what she has to say. I know you want to believe what she did was spiteful, but it wasn't the case at all. When you get out of your feelings, sit down and talk to her."

"Nah, I'm good."

"MICKEY!!!!!" Stop acting like that. This woman was about to be your wife. She birthed two kids for you. She loved you and still does, even after you gave her diseases and cheated on her. The least you could do is hear her out. You owe her that much."

"Yea whatever." He hung the phone up in my ear.

"It's ok sis. He's hurting too. I'll be around when he wants to talk." I didn't know she was standing there.

38

"Yea but this back and forth shit is stupid and he knows it. That man loves the ground you walk on. He just can't get out of his own way to give you what you want, and he knows you deserve."

"I know. He told me the night of the accident." She smiled.

"You saw him?"

"Yea, he came and kidnapped me from the party."

"Bitch, you fucked him." She laughed shaking her head.

"Of course I did. No matter what we're going through, he's still the love of my life. He's my soul mate, even if he chose another. I don't wish no ill will to him or whatever woman he ends up with. I just don't care for Faith, that's all."

"So you're telling me, if he decided to be with another woman besides her, you would be ok with that?"

"I would never be ok with him lying down with another, but I have to respect the decision he makes, just like I would expect him to do the same."

"Bitch you're crazy as hell if you think my brother will allow you to sleep with any other man now that you had two of his kids. You are his baby momma and no other kids will leave your body unless they're by him."

"You're crazy." She waved me off.

"No, I'm serious. He may be with others, but he won't have more then one woman to have his kids."

"Faith almost did."

"Yea, but that was a slip up and you can guarantee he won't allow it to happen twice."

"Yea well. I'm done having kids for now. These two are only months apart." She pointed to Jr. who was playing with a toy and Joy, who was on my moms lap.

"I know. Ricardo is ready for another one. Once we find out who's behind this, I'm going to give him another one. Who knows, maybe we'll be in a race to see who has ten kids first."

"Ten kids? Bitch you're bugging."

"Oh you don't want that many?" I questioned as if ten was a small amount.

"Hell no." She yelled and I laughed.

"Shit, I do. I want all my kids to have a huge family and be able to depend on each other when we're gone."

"Yea, I'm good on that."

"That's what you say now but don't underestimate my brother. He will try and put as many in you as possible." She burst out laughing.

"Bye girl. I'm going to lie down. Oh, do you think you can stop by Miguel's' house and pick some of my clothes from there? I should have a few things still there brand new if the bitch hasn't tried it on."

"Yea, I'll go now. You sure you don't want to come with me?"

"No. When I get this cast and sling off, then I'll go." She said smirking. I knew what that meant. I sent a message to my brother letting him know I was on my way to get some things for Violet, but he didn't text back.

****

I parked behind his truck and went inside. I didn't hear or see anyone, so I went to the bedroom and found a suitcase in his closet. V was right, she still had mad shit with tags on it in here. I knew they didn't belong to Faith because her tacky ass didn't know how to dress.

I packed as much as I could and went into the baby's room. He still had stuff in bags from the birthday party, so I packed that up too. Joy would be ok until we went to the store tomorrow.

I walked down the steps and Faith was coming out of my brothers' office with a smirk on her face. That's why I didn't hear shit because the office is sound proof.

"So you came for her shit huh?" She asked with her arms folded.

"Yup. It sucks to be staying here and still see all of her things exactly how she left it. It's like he knows she's coming back."

"What the fuck ever. She isn't coming back to this house. He don't want her ass after she kept the baby a secret."

"Who told you that shit Faith?" He yelled causing her to jump. He had scratches on the side of his face and it looked like his eye was red.

"Told me what?"

42

"Who told you Violet kept a baby from me?" She backed up until she hit the wall.

"I over heard you talking on the phone earlier." I glanced at my brother who seemed to be in deep thought like he couldn't remember it.

"I don't remember saying that to anyone." She looked shook.

"Whatever, who cares? It's out there now." Miguel shook his head and stared at me.

"Did you get enough stuff for her and my son?" He asked.

"Yea. It's still a lot left in there."

"It can stay there." I smirked at Faith who was fuming in the corner.

"Let me talk to you Mickey?" She started walking behind us.

"Alone bitch. Now move." I pushed her back and closed the front door in her face.

"What Hazel? I don't want to here any shit. I'm fine."

"Mickey you're not fine. This shit right here is not ok." I pointed to the scratches and black eye.

"I won't hit her Hazel." He helped me place the stuff in my car.

"Fuck that. I will."

"I know but it's fine."

"Mickey, I love you to death but if you don't get this under control, she's going to kill you. I'm telling you the bitch is sneaky and she's up to something."

"She ain't doing shit." Just like a man to underestimate a woman.

"Miguel, I'm hungry can we go get something to eat?" She opened the door and stood there waiting.

"Violet would never treat you like this." I whispered in his ear and pulled off.

****

"I didn't mean to go there with him but the beatings on my brother are getting worse and worse. I know he feels like it's nothing because he's a man, but this shit is out of control.

44

Every time I see him there's a new mark on him." I told my mother.

"What do you mean a new mark?" Violet and my mom both stared at me waiting for an answer.

"Three weeks ago, I stopped by before Jr.'s party and he had burns on his arm. I asked him what happened, he told me, he walked into the iron. I know that's a lie because he's been getting his clothes dry cleaned for years."

"Fuck this sling and this cast. Take me over there right now. I'm about to beat this bitch's ass." Violet yelled out with tears streaming down her face.

"V. There's nothing we can do honey. She's been doing this to him for years and he takes up for her. I think he feels bad for her, that's why he keeps going back to her.

"Why would he feel bad for her?"

"When she was 15, she was raped by her dad. It went on for a few years but when she met Miguel, she thought her prayers were answered. She knew he was a bad boy and he'd say something to her dad and make him stop. Unfortunately, her dad didn't give a fuck about Miguel and since Faith never

45

told my son; the rape continued. Her mom knew and let it happen.

One night he was raping her, and Miguel stopped by. Her mom and sister opened the door and pointed to the room she was in. He went in and found the dad on top of her and shot him right on the spot. He had Faith come stay with us for a while until he found her a place to stay.

She didn't like that Miguel would be out all hours of the night while she was home with us, so she went back home and only came over when he was there. That's when the fighting started and the first time, she hit him was when he got 15 stitches for cheating on her. The beatings never stopped; she would cry and apologize, and he would feel bad for her. I think he's become so immune to the shit, he allows it.

Violet my son doesn't know what real love is because this is the shit he's dealt with, dealing with her. Then you came in and stole his heart, showed him what real love was, gave him two kids and planned on marrying him. When you left him, he didn't know what to do with his self. You were and still are everything to him." Violet looked at her.

"Yes he cheated but you were his BOSS BITCH."
When I heard my mom break it down, I knew what she meant
all those years ago when she tried to explain to me.

"I didn't want to be a BOSS BITCH. I just wanted to be
with him."

"Honey he knows and it's why he's so in love with you.
The secret you held, hurt him. He missed out on her birth and
even if it was recorded, it's not the same. He has you on a
pedal stool and he refuses to take you off." Violet started
crying.

"All I'm saying is when he asked you to wait for him
that night in the hotel, it wasn't to fuck others. It was to get his
mind right. He's not used to love. All he's known is being in
an abusive relationship and he believes the shit is healthy."

"I love him too, but I can't sit around and watch her do
this to him either. What if she tries to kill him?"

"I pray it doesn't happen but only he knows when
enough is enough. It's like a battered woman; he's a battered
man." My mom told her and got up to cook.

I ended up staying over to have a girl's night with them.

Ricardo came by around midnight and we had sex in the truck.

I knew he was missing me and the feelings were the same but I

needed to handle this shit with my brother and he understood.

If he wanted his wife to fuck him and suck him off, then he got

it with no questions asked no matter where I am.

Miguel

It's been two months since I found out I had a daughter. The day I found out; a nigga was hurt like a motherfucker. I never thought I'd miss the day any of my kids were born. I've seen the kids' everyday at my moms though. V would stay in the room when I was there, and I was fine with that. She was selfish as hell for doing it and today I was going to hear her side of the story.

I gave my mom the keys to the house I originally had built for her which was only a half hour away from me. It was fully furnished but she and my sister still went out to get sheets, dishes and other odds and ends as Hazel called it. No one knew about this spot but my mom, my sister, her husband and me. I wasn't taking any chances of someone trying to kill her again. Her shit had surveillance like she was the president too.

I put the code to her gate in and parked my car behind hers. I got her the 2016 champagne Porsche truck she asked for fully loaded with TV's and all that for the kids. Of course, it was bulletproof too.

I stepped inside and saw my niece and son in the living room playing with toys and watching TV. I walked in further and saw my daughter in the nanny's lap as she tried to feed her. She looked just like her mother, but she was stubborn just like me. It was the opposite with my son: he looked just like me but was kind and loving like his mom. She made him soft but I was changing that.

Violet was on the phone with her back turned cooking. She spun around and jumped.

"You scared me Miguel." She told whoever was on the phone she would call them back." I asked after smelling the aroma.

"I made a ham, baked macaroni and cheese, collard greens, baked beans and some corn bread with a chocolate cake." I grinned when she said it. She knew it was my favorite.

"Who you making all this food for? And on a Friday."

"No one. I was homesick and your mom didn't feel like making it for me, so Karen an I cooked."

"It's done if you want a plate." Karen was already making small plates for the kids. I fixed myself one and sat

50

down to eat. V sat down at the kitchen table helping Jr. and my niece eat the best she could. Her arm must be bothering her.

"Where's your sling at?"

"Miguel, that's been off the first week we got back. The doctor didn't want my arm getting stiff, so I only wear it in bed."

"What about your collar bone?"

"He said it's healing quickly, and physical therapy starts next week. I need to regain full use of my arm. I'm happy though. I've been trying to move it more and more everyday but it's still tender."

"Are you going to bust the stitches?"

"Boy you haven't been around me in a long time. The stitches are out and again, the doctor said it's healing well." I felt stupid because all the times I've stopped at my moms, neither one of us wanted to see each other and I never checked on her. Today was the first day, I was face to face with her.

She dyed her hair some burgundy shit and cut it down to her shoulders. She lost a little weight, but she was still perfect to me.

I finished eating and helped her and Karen with the kids.

I stayed and gave them a bath and watched that damn Frozen

again. I'm throwing the DVD out when I leave. I refuse to

make my eyes watch another hour and a half of it.

We put the kids to bed around 8:30 and Karen went to

the other part of the house. She was a live-in nanny, so she had

her own entrance and privacy. I locked up and went to find

Violet.

After dinner she disappeared and let me spend time

with the kids. She was knocked out on her bed with the TV still

on. I went to put the covers on her, and she popped up.

"Hey. Are you leaving?"

"Yea. I wanted to talk but we can do it another time."

"No it's fine. Let me take a quick shower I smell like

food. That's what I came to do earlier but once I sat down, I

was out." She laughed. I could hear sounds, so I stepped inside.

I found her in the shower with her knees to her chest.

"What's wrong V?" She was shaking and crying. Her

not answering, caused me to panic. I dialed my moms' number;

I figured she would know what's going on since she had been

staying with her.

"Ma something's wrong with Violet."

"Tell me what she's doing." I explained to my mom and she told me that Violet had been having flashbacks about the accident and the shooting. Her anxiety was at an all time high and sometimes she had black outs. When she thought about it, she kept thinking about losing me and the kids.

My mom told me where she kept the pills and to make her take one. After a few minutes, she snapped out of it and stood up to wash herself. I didn't know what to do or say. I just stood there watching her.

"Miguel can you scrub under this arm for me? Karen usually helps me but you're here."

"Give me the rag. Yo, who's been shaving you?" I asked noticing she had a fresh one down there and her arms and legs were too.

"I shave myself fool. Karen helps with this arm because it's hard for me to lift that's all. Why do you care anyway?" I put my head down. She was right. Who am I to question her when I have my own shit going on?

53

I helped her out the shower and wrapped a towel around her. She sat on her bed and I took the lotion and rubbed it on her body. I missed everything about her and seeing her a little helpless was weighing heavy on me. I should be taking care of her.

"What did you want to talk about?" She stood up and put on one of my t-shirts.

"Where did you get this from?"

"Oh. I had Hazel grab me a few the day she got my stuff from your house. You know I love sleeping in your shirts. Do you want it back?"

"No. I want you back though." I said forgetting I just asked her a question. Being in her presence had me wanting to stay forever.

"Don't do this to me Miguel."

"Don't do what? Say, I miss the hell out of you or how I feel like shit that I can't be here for you." I stared at her.

"Violet, I love you so much and I know I hurt you but I need you and my kids in my life."

"Just tell me why you fucked her and was she the only

54

one?" I ran my hand down my face before I answered.

"She was the only one at first." Violet rolled her eyes.

"When you left me, I started going out and I hit a few others off. Why did I fuck her? To be honest; just because I could."

"Because you could?" She scoffed up a laugh.

"I went to the house to kill her, she came out the shower with a towel wrapped around her. It dropped, my dick got hard, she sucked it, and I fucked her and left. I continued fucking her because you let me." I saw how pissed she got when I said that.

"What the fuck you mean I let you?"

"V the first day I slept with her and came home, I saw the hickey she left on my neck, so I know you did. You didn't say anything; I left it alone. The next few times she did the same thing and again no response from you. I figured you didn't care and was ok with it as long as I brought my ass home to you." She remained quiet.

"The night you left, I knew you were done with me. I saw it in your eyes, and I heard it in your voice. I told myself you weren't strong enough to stay away but you were. That's when I knew I fucked up and you weren't coming back."

"Miguel, I love you too and I've been missing you like crazy but I can't live like that. I know you're the *"Connect"* but I still don't want my man out there sexing all these bitches and coming home to me like it's ok. I'm dying inside thinking about how you made love to those women."

"Let me stop you right there. I've never made love to anyone but you. I don't kiss these chicks, nor do I go down on them. You are the only and will remain the only woman in my life to get that."

"Yea right. And what about Faith?"

"What about her. I've gone down on her a few times in the last couple of years but that's not what she's into. Don't get me wrong, she loves it but she's more of a fuck and suck your dick type of chick. I think the things she's been through deterred her away from wanting it done to her. I'm good with that; she was a screamer when I did it and she got on my nerves." I saw Violet grinning.

"You're not right."

"Well she was." I shrugged.

"Anyway, come find me when you're ready to settle down. I'm not going anywhere. The kids have me doing too much to even think about trying to be with someone else." She pulled the covers up.

"What did I tell you in the hotel room? You're mine and I better not find out you let anyone close enough to even smell your perfume." I kissed her gently and she grabbed my face with her hands the best she could. Our tongues ignited a fire we knew was going to take us to a place we couldn't turn back from.

I slid my hand between her legs and felt her juices leaking out. I stuck two fingers inside and brought them back out to put in my mouth.

"You still taste how Papi remembers."

"Mmmmm, then Papi needs to clean up the mess he made down there." I licked my lips, took my shirt off, spread her legs open and ate her pussy like it was my last time. I had her screaming so loud I made her put a pillow over her head. Nothing could prepare me for the feeling I got when I entered her.

Her pussy latched on to my dick so tight, I came right away. It didn't even bother her. She had me stand up on the side of the bed and gave me some of her bomb ass head. I didn't want her to swallow my kids because I planned on getting her pregnant again; Tonight.

I made love to her all night long. Neither one of us made a remark about me pulling out. The last time I emptied my seeds in her, she pulled me tighter and told me I just got her pregnant. I think we both wanted another baby.

"I love you Violet and I swear I'm going to make it up to you." I had a few tears leaving my eyes. I never had a woman make me cry but the way her pussy felt and my emotions together, a nigga was definitely in his feelings. She just kissed them away and told me she loved me too.

"We're getting married in the morning Violet." I kissed her forehead while she slept on my chest. I was not letting her get away this time. I just had to figure out how I would get rid of Faith.

Violet

"Yes Senor. The dress should fit." I heard talking all around me, but I knew no one was in my house. I glanced at the clock and it was 6:30 in the damn morning; on a Saturday too. I saw three women standing in my room. One had a tape measure going around my body, another one was taking out all these hair and makeup products and the other one was taking a dress out of a bag hanging up.

"What the hell is going on? And why are you in my room? Matter of fact, who let you in my house?" Hazel came bursting through the door chippy as ever.

"Come on girl, we do not have all day." She helped me get out of bed and had me get in the shower.

"What is going on Hazel? And where are the kids?" I shouted from the bathroom.

"Girl your mom and dad came and took the kids when you were sleep last night."

"My mom and dad. What the hell? What are they doing in Puerto Rico?" I questioned because I didn't call them.

"Girl stop playing. Mickey said he told you." She yelled out to me n the bathroom.

"Told me what?" I asked when she came in and helped me lift my arm to wash.

"Violet, you're getting married in a few hours." I smiled because I do remember him saying it. I just thought he was caught up in the moment.

"Why are you smiling?"

"No reason. How did he set all this up?"

"You worry too much about the details. I just have to get you to the church by 1:00. His nasty ass said he wants to be inside you on the jet by midnight."

"Are you serious?" Miguel really had no filter.

"Yes. I can't with him." When we came out the bathroom my sisters, niece, and a bunch of damn kids were there.

"Bitch, the next time you make up with him, do it early. He had us getting out of bed at one o clock in the morning." One of the ladies brought the dress over for me to see it.

The dress was strapless with rhinestones or diamonds

draped in the middle. It was low cut in the back with a fishtail train. The veil had a tiara at the top with diamonds all through it. Ang told me he had the dress made when he proposed the first time.

The girls all wore baby blue strapless bridesmaid dresses and their hair, jewelry and shoes were all the same.

The limo pulled up to the church at exactly one and to say cars were lined up everywhere was an understatement. There were dark Suburban's everywhere, diplomat cars, and cops had to direct traffic. I felt like the First Lady with all these people here.

The wedding started and once again, I had an eerie feeling but I wasn't worried because the security was extra tight. The church was packed to capacity and everyone stood when the doors opened for me. I walked down the aisle to the song Lets Get Married (the slow version) by Jagged Edge. I saw Miguel wipe a few tears as I tried to hold my own in. I failed as soon as he lifted my veil. The tears came racing down so fast I couldn't catch them.

The ceremony was perfect as we both said our own

vows. We jumped the broom because this fool said he watched the movie and wanted to do it.

The reception was at some ballroom that held over 1000 people. I was introduced to so many people from different parts of P.R, the U.S., other countries and his cousins Cream and Darius from Jersey.

"You look beautiful. My cousin got him a bad chick." His cousin Darius said as he hugged me. I thought Miguel was going to flip but he smiled.

"Girl don't worry, he's not going to kill us. We know how he is about people making compliments to his woman. We like fucking with him." Cream said laughing.

They introduced me to their wives who seemed to be cool. They offered us to come stay with them whenever Miguel lets me out of his sight.

"I have a surprise for my brother and new sister in law." Hazel spoke on the mic. I looked at Miguel who shrugged his shoulders.

"My brother told me this was going to be the song for their first dance. So I decided, what better way then to get them both here to sing it to them."

The song *I've Changed* came on by Keyshia Cole and Jahiem who both came out singing. Miguel grabbed my hand, and everyone cleared the dance floor. We were enjoying the song but when the last verse came on, he had my back against his chest while they sung the part.

New and improved, you bring out the best in me,

because the old me, was lonely, searching for my one

and only,

so happy that I found you.

Saw the potential, and you made it so simple to be

loved

And I'll never be the same, baby for you I've changed.

The next song came on and I swear if I didn't ever hear it again, it would be too soon. Future's song Neva End played. We danced the rest of the night away before saying our goodbyes to everyone. My mom and dad were staying in P.R. to help with the kids until we came back.

Our honeymoon was in Fiji on a private island called Kanacea that he informed me he purchased for us. It was only 3,000 acres and had one house on it. It had white sand, palm trees, the weather was perfect, and it was on the Pacific Ocean.

Miguel and I stayed for two weeks before I started getting homesick. I missed my babies and he had to get back to his business even though its been running smoothly. Him and Butch were on the phone daily discussing everything.

"V, you know you're pregnant right?" He rubbed my stomach.

"Probably." We both laughed as the jet came down for landing. Hazel met us with the kids and my parents. The jet was going to fuel up and take them home right after.

"Take care of my daughter." My dad said pulling him in for a hug.

"Without a doubt." He kissed my mom on the cheek, and we talked until it was time for them to leave. The drive home was the a little over and hour since my place was further then everyone else's.

"Are you staying in tonight?" I asked Miguel who was

laid out on the bed.

"Yea. It's back to business tomorrow."

"Why? Are you going to miss me?" He asked grinning.

"I miss you when you go to the bathroom baby." I climbed on top of him.

"Damn. I got you strung out like that?"

"Whatever Miguel. I have something to tell you." He muted the TV and sat up.

"What's wrong?"

"The day of our wedding when I was getting ready to walk in the church, I felt like someone was watching me."

"Why didn't you mention it to me?"

"I knew nothing would happen because of all the security but now that we're back, I want to make sure you're aware."

"V, I'll die before I let anything happen to you. I couldn't protect you when you had the accident because you ran from me, but I promise not to let anyone hurt you again."

"So, I'm really the BOSS BITCH now huh?" He smiled and moved closer to me.

"You are definitely the boss but stop calling yourself a bitch."

"That's what your mom said I was."

"I know it's what women call themselves when they have powerful men. Is that what you want to be called?"

"Let me think about it." I laid back in between his legs watching some bullshit on ESPN. I felt him move me over and put the covers on me. He hugged me from behind and fell asleep no too long after. If this is what I'm about to spend the rest of my life doing, I'll take it.

Miguel

Two weeks ago, I married the woman of my dreams and I wouldn't change anything about it. She is and will always be the only woman I'll love and its only right to make her Mrs. Rodriguez.

I got up around ten and noticed my wife wasn't in the bed. Wow, even saying my wife is weird but I'm sure I'll get used to it. I hopped in the shower and threw on some jeans, a t-shirt and Jordan's. I was going to my house to let Faith know this shit was over. I know V wouldn't be too happy about it but she has to trust me at some point.

"Good morning baby." I kissed her neck while she made me a plate.

"Good morning to you too." She handed me a glass of orange juice. I saw her go in the living room and put on a pair of Jordan's too. Hazel walked in wearing some sweats and sneakers.

"Ok, what the hell are you two up to?"

"Oh, we're going with you to kick Faith's ass out." I spit my orange juice out.

"We can't come." Violet walked in my direction licking her lips. She stood in between my legs and stuck her hands down my jeans and kissed my neck.

"Stop playing V before I take you back in the room."

"We can go in the room but I'm still coming with you." I took her hand out because my man was waking up.

I grabbed my keys and her hand and walked out the front door. I told my sister to take her car because Violet would need a ride home after wards. I stuck my hands down her pants.

"Oh you think you're the only one who can play those games?"

"No baby. But right now, I'm the only one that can do this." She moved my hand, made my dick disappear in her mouth and I almost crashed. I drove slow but not too slow for anyone to think something was wrong.

"Shit, V. I'm about to cum."

"Mmmmm go ahead. You know I love the way you taste." Soon as she said it, I released in her mouth. She made sure to catch everything.

"Sit back and spread them legs for me." She lifted her self up, took her pants down and stuck my finger inside. She fucked them like it was my dick. I was rock hard again. I turned to kiss her and she grabbed my man back out and jerked him off.

"Miguel, I'm cumming baby. Don't stop." I felt her release on my hand. I sucked all her juices off and pulled her closer for a kiss.

"I love the fuck out of you girl."

"I love you more."

"You know I'm fucking the shit out of you later?"

"That's what I want. If Hazel wasn't behind us, I would've told you to pull over already. I need to feel that dick inside me right now." Her bottom half was still naked. I hit the Bluetooth to call my sister.

"What, you fucking freaks? I know yall up there being nasty." We just started laughing.

"I'm about to pull over for a few minutes; meet me at the house."

"Bye." She rode by blowing the horn and sticking up her middle finger. We were on a dirt rode and no one comes down it much.

"Baby ride your dick." She hopped on and both of us came within minutes. I wanted to fuck some more but her shoulder started hurting.

"Are you sure you're ok?"

"Yea baby. It's just too tight in here. I probably hit it on something."

"That's what you get for being a freak."

"I'm only a freak for you."

"You better be." We drove off hand in hand to my house.

We got to my house and Faith's car was there and my sister was sitting in the car with her face turned up when she saw us.

"I can't stand y'all." She said flipping us the bird again.

"That's not nice Hazel."

"Whatever V. Neither was watching him almost crash a few times."

"Aww you were worried?" I said putting her in the headlock.

"Get off me. I do not need to smell Violet's pussy on me."

"Shit, I do. It makes my day."

"Ughhh just forget it." She put her key in the door and Faith stood there with her arms folded.

"What are they doing here?" She rolled her eyes.

"Faith lets go to my office. I need to talk to you." I turned around and kissed V on her lips.

"Baby do you trust me?" I asked her. I knew she had a problem with me taking her in my office because its sound proof.

"Yes. But I swear to God if she puts her hands on you, I'm whooping her ass."

"That's my baby. But you know I'm not letting you fight with my baby in your stomach."

"Be quiet and go handle your business." I stepped into my office where Faith was already sitting. I noticed a few tears falling down her face and to be honest, I didn't care anymore. She used to get me with those all the time but now that I know what its like to be in a healthy relationship, I was over it.

My computer was on and it looked like scratch marks were on my desk drawers like someone was trying to get in them. Thank goodness all my important shit stayed at my sister's house.

We stared at one another, waiting for the other to speak first. I looked down at my phone that went off. I opened it up and it was a pussy shot of Violet upstairs in one of the bathrooms. That woman had me crazy in love with her ass. I sent her back a message telling her to keep it wet.

"Well."

"Well what?" I asked closing my phone up.

"Why are they here?"

"Look Faith. Our relationship has run its course. There's no more me and you."

"What? You're just leaving me again?" She began getting upset.

"Faith cut the shit. You know I got married two weeks ago because your ass was watching Violet walk in the church." She rolled her eyes which let me know that's probably who she felt staring at her.

"Miguel, how are you just going to marry this chick and you wouldn't marry me?"

"Faith, you never had my heart and you had a hand problem. You know I told you over and over about it, but you didn't stop."

"Miguel, I'll stop please don't do this."

"Faith, you're bugging. I'm already married."

"Are you still going to take care of me?"

"You must be trying to make my wife kill me. There's no way in hell I would do that."

"Oh she runs you?"

"Nah, but she's my BOSS BITCH so if you need something from me, you need to go through her."

"Come on Miguel. I know we can think of something."
She stood up and lifted her shirt over her head. I admit the shit
used to turn me on but now that I'm married, I wouldn't
disrespect V like that. She tried to put her hands in my jeans,
and I grabbed her wrist.

"Goodbye Faith." She stood there looking stupid. I
went to open the door and felt her hand across my face. I was
praying Violet didn't hear but my prayers weren't answered
because she came out of nowhere and pounced on Faith.

"Bitch are you crazy putting your hands on my
husband? He won't hit you, but I will." She screamed as I
lifted her up.

Faith stood up with blood leaking down her face. V
fucked her up good just that fast. I could see how embarrassed
Faith was, but she brought it on herself. She headed for the
front door but Hazel stopped her to hand her two bags with
clothes in them I guess.

"Don't bring your ass back here." She left out looking
stupid and broken.

"Miguel, I think my shoulder may have slipped out or something."

"Why you say that?" I was inspecting her shoulder.

"It hurts a lot." I had her raise it.

"I told your ass not to fight her. You probably strained it. You haven't been to therapy yet because we went straight on our honeymoon."

"Fuck that. I heard her smack you. Don't nobody put their hands on my man but me."

"Damn V. I swear you can look at me and my dick gets hard. But when you get like this, it makes me want to strip you right here, right now."

"Oh hell no. You two are not about to fuck with me in this house."

"Relax sis. Your brother will never get a taste of my pussy in this house again." I gave her this crazy ass look. She stepped in front of me.

"Get rid of this house Miguel. I want to see it on the market in the morning."

"Huh? I love this house."

"You're going to build us a bigger and better house. At the rate we're going it's going to be needed anyway." She grabbed my dick and I knew she meant from all the fucking we do.

"You got that." We stayed around the house packing up only the things I needed. Everything could be replaced. The chef and maids were going to start at Violets house next week until the new one is built. This was my life and I loved it. I kissed V goodbye as she sat in my sisters' car and went to my office.

Faith

This bitch must've lost her mind if she thinks I was allowing her to sail off into the sunset with my man. Miguel and I were meant to be together whether it's love or not. I worked too damn hard to be with him and no tramp from the states is taking him away.

Miguel saved me from my dad years ago and even though I thanked him tons of times, I feel like I will always owe him. Miguel is such a good man but when he makes me mad, I can't control myself. I know beating on a man is no better if it were the other way around. I watched my mom do it to my dad every time he finished having sex with me. In my opinion she should've killed him for doing it instead of hitting him.

The first time he did it, my mom went to the store and he made me come in the room with him. I didn't think anything of it because he was my dad and I was daddy's girl.

"Baby girl your body is filling out more and more each day." I felt uncomfortable when he said it but didn't pay much

77

mind to it.

"I know dad, mom tells me all the time." Nothing else was said after that.

One Friday night my mom stayed at work late and my sister spent the night at her friends' house. My little friend who was a boy walked me home and kissed my cheek. My dad saw him and pulled me inside.

"Oh, you're letting boys kiss you. What else are you letting them do?"

"Nothing daddy." He snatched my arm, took me in my room and tossed me on the bed.

"Let me see if you've been touched." I didn't know how he was going to find that out. He yanked my pants and panties down.

"Spread those legs."

"Daddy no one touched me. I'm a virgin."

"I'll be the judge of that." He put his face in between my legs. I started crying as he stuck one finger inside. I jumped back on the bed.

"Hmmm seems like you are." He said licking his fingers.

78

I was disgusted. I went to reach for my clothes, and he pushed me back down.

I need to taste it now."

"What?" I screamed out. He put his hand on my mouth and his tongue flickered on my pussy. I cried so hard until a feeling of pleasure took over my body. I didn't know what was happening, but I was embarrassed. My dad started moving my hips against his face and when I looked down, he was jerking his dick with his face inside my pussy. The feeling made my entire body jerk.

He stood up and forcefully entered me until he came. I felt violated and the hurt was evident in my moms' eyes as she watched him take my innocence in front of her.

This happened for years until I met Miguel who was my lifesaver. It took me a while to enjoy sex with Miguel, but he took his time and showed me the true meaning of sex. I don't think he ever made love to me because I only wanted to fuck. He gave me oral sex and had me climbing walls and screaming. I wanted him to do it more, but he doesn't because he pleases me in other ways.

I have to come up with a plan to send this bitch back to America and quick. It's going to be harder since he married her. The one thing he's always told me was when he found the right woman to marry, he would never cheat on her no matter how bad the bitch was. Marriage was sacred to him; especially, after watching what his parents went through.

"What's up? I haven't heard from you since that shit a couple months back. Good job by the way, but you missed."

"Don't worry about that. Just make sure you hold up your end of the bargain with his cousins out in Jersey. I'm already out here fucking their shit up now, but I want to make sure I end up on top."

"You know I got your back. But listen I have to go. Hit me up when you're on the way here."

"Ok see you soon. Make sure you got that dick checked. The last time you burnt me."

"My bad. I guess I ran up in the wrong one raw."

"Ugh ya think." I hung the phone up on him and stepped in my moms' house. Miguel killed my family and the only thing I have left, is this house and two bags of clothes. I really need to re evaluate my life.

"Hey you." He answered on the third ring.

"Faith is that you?"

"Yup the one and only."

"I see you're no longer the BOSS BITCH to the infamous Miguel Rodriguez."

"Who told you that?" He laughed in the phone.

"No one told me. I was at the wedding and that pretty bitch was not you under the veil. What happened? I thought we had this?"

"Shit me too. I'm still down. We just have to come up with a new plan."

"We, my ass. You should've fucked him better to keep him." The guy said on the phone.

"Shut up. Anyway, I have a plan in motion already. Just wait."

"Ok don't take too long. That offer only last until the end of the year and that's two months away."

"I got you. I'll call you when it's done." I hung up with him and started calculating my next move.

Hazel

"Miguel something isn't right with Faith." I told my brother a few days after we all kicked her out the house.

"Sis don't start. I don't need Violet hurting herself again on some nonsense you talking about Faith's stupid ass by fighting."

"I'm serious Miguel. When have you noticed Faith to get into a fight and walk out without talking shit; or at least threatening someone? She is up to something and I'm going to find out what it is." I hung the phone up on my brother because as usual, his ass was in denial about the crazy bitch.

I didn't want to get on his bad side because he was just starting to forgive me for hiding Violet and keeping his daughter a secret. I though he was going to kill me when my mom told him. I swear if Ricardo wasn't there, I could see him choking the life out of me. I've only seen him that mad with people who crossed him so when he looked at me with the same face, I thought it was over.

I went over to Violet's house because I knew if I

couldn't get him to believe me; she would. I'm not saying it was the right thing to do knowing how overprotective she is of him but at least she'll watch his back. When I got there, she was on the phone, so I laid on the bed waiting for her to her off.

"What's up bitch"

"Nothing. Who was that on the phone?" I asked being nosy.

"Oh that was my ex Dom." I was shocked at how nonchalant she was about speaking with him.

"You still talk to him?" I gave her the side eye.

"Yea. We've always had that best friend type of relationship. I used to write him when he was in jail and visit, but he told me not to put my life on hold. I still tried to after he told me not, but my letters would come back, and he took me off his visitation list. I didn't understand why at first, but I get it. If he didn't, I probably would've never met my husband, so I thank him every time we speak for that."

"Girl you're crazy. Does Mickey know?"

"No not yet. It's not like I'm hiding the fact we still communicate. I just want him to know we're strictly friends.

Telling him right now would be too much, being I told him to cut Faith off."

I understood what she was saying but he wouldn't. He hated keeping secrets; especially, since the biggest one she held is almost six months old.

"I don't know sis. I think you should tell him."

"Ok fine. Look I'm sending him a text right now"

She handed me the phone and it said, *hey baby I was thinking about you. Just wanted to let you know my ex Dom called and I spoke to him a few times. Didn't want to keep secrets I love you."*

"Are you happy now?"

"Girl you didn't have to do that for me. But you know my brothers going to ask why didn't you tell him about the first time he called? But hey you're grown."

"Anyway, party pooper what brings you over here?"

I started telling her what my feelings were regarding the way Faith was acting and she agreed. We both came up with some of the weird shit she was doing and decided to follow her ass tomorrow.

""She was too quick to give Miguel up without a fight that day. There's no way she would allow another woman to take her spot. That's all I'm saying." I told V.

We were still discussing it, when we heard a door slam. I sat closer to the headboard because I knew my brother was coming home after he read the text she sent.

"Hazel can you step out for a minute?" I glanced over at V who looked scared to death.

"Ugh no she can stay in here. How are you going to tell my company to leave?"

He gave me this look and I high tailed it out of there. I love Violet but I wasn't about to be on the end of that shit storm. I grabbed my stuff and left. I ran smack dab into Ricardo who was getting out the truck.

"Hey baby."

"Don't hey baby me Hazel."

"Huh?"

"Don't play dumb. I hope you didn't know she was keeping that secret too." He said grabbing my waist.

"I swear baby, this time I didn't know. I'm the one who

made her text Miguel."

"You think she fucking with her ex?" He asked.

"No. The conversation was definitely a friend like one. I think they're just catching up on each other's life that's all. But she shouldn't have kept it from Miguel."

"He knew already."

"If he knew, why is he acting like he didn't?"

"He only knew about the time she saw him at the club when he went to the states, an a few times after. He didn't know she was still talking to him after they got married."

"He said this must've been the first time she talked to him since, because her phone records don't have any indication of them speaking."

"Damn. I wonder why now?"

"Babe there's always a motive for people who come back into your life whether they were in jail or not. I'm not saying he's trying to get her back but he's definitely staying in touch with her for a reason. Your brother doesn't know why and he's going to protect his family no matter what the cost."

"Well I'm leaving because I don't want no parts of that

shit."

"Ok. I'll see you at home." I gave him a kiss and went to my car.

"Oh and Hazel."

"Yea babe." I turned around.

"Have that pussy wet when I get home tonight. It's been a minute since I felt you."

"Baby we had sex two days ago."

"Exactly two days, too long."

"Be safe. I love you."

"I love you too." I pulled off laughing at his crazy ass. But that's my man and I love him to death. Now if I can figure out what Faith is up to, we can all sleep better?

Miguel

"Violet what the fuck?" I could tell she was nervous about answering. She started tearing up and I didn't know why.

"What you about to cry for?" I asked her while I leaned against the dresser with my arms folded.

"Because you in here yelling at me like I did something wrong." She said with a straight face.

"Let me get this right. You can talk to your ex and I can't?"

"Miguel your situation with her is different then mine."

"Oh yea. Tell me how?"

"For one, I'm not sleeping with him. Two… he lives in another country and three, I don't want him." She came to where I was standing and rubbed her hand down my face.

"V, you're grown an I don't want you to think I'm trying to tell you what to do or who to talk to, but don't you think something is fishy with him?"

"What do you mean?"

"Ok he just got out of jail and hadn't spoken to you in

years. Yes, he was looking for you but why? Why now? There's a motive behind every move he's making baby. I know you don't want to believe it but there is."

"But why?"

"V. You don't think he knows who you're married to? I know you don't think it has anything to do with me but you're wrong. The nigga wants something."

"Well he isn't getting it from me."

"I'm not doubting you baby. I trust you to the fullest. It's these niggas out here I have to watch. All I'm asking is that you respect your man."

"I do respect you Miguel."

"I know you do but I'm asking you to cut ties with him until I find out what's going on with him. If there's nothing, then I'm cool with you speaking to him every now and then. I just need to be sure. Can you do that for me?"

"Yes baby. I won't talk to him until you find out." She put her arms around my waist.

"Good. Now get packed."

"Huh? Packed for what?"

"We're going to Jersey."

"Now."

"Yes. We're only staying two days. I have a few meetings out there and I want you with me." The good thing about having your own jet is, you can up and go when you please.

"Fine. What time are we leaving?"

"Two hours."

"Two hours? I'm going to kill you Miguel."

"I love you too baby." I smacked her ass and walked out.

****

The ride to Jersey was a quiet one because Violet slept the entire way. I know she's probably pregnant again but I'm gonna wait for her to tell me. My son was almost two and Joy wasn't even one yet. I had her popping out babies back to back. Oh well at least we'll get them out the way.

"We're here baby. Wake up." I lifted her head off my lap and waited for the doors to open.

I dropped her off at the hotel and went to my meeting

with a few distributors. I was supposed to meet up with my two cousins Cream and Darius but neither one of them has been answering their phone since the wedding.

After my meeting, I had V meet me out for dinner. I told her to wear something nice but when she showed up, I wanted her ass to go back to the room. Now I see what she meant when she said, after I get dressed she doesn't want anyone to see me.

My wife wore a short navy blue fitted dress that had a criss cross over the chest area. She showed off her long sexy ass legs with some strap up red bottoms. Her hair was parted down the middle but straight and she had on little makeup. I could see the men at the table hawking over her.

"Hey baby." She pecked me on the lips and then used her finger to wipe off any lip-gloss. All the men stood up and waited for her to take a seat. I introduced her to everyone there and had the waitress take her order since we had done so already.

"That's a beautiful ring you have and you are stunning." One of the guys' side chicks sitting next to her said. Yes, she was his side chick because his wife was at the wedding with him and this ain't her.

"Thank you. My husband treats me well."

"I see." The bitch had the nerve to look at me and lick her lips.

The shit happened so fast that no one knew what happened until it was over. Violet had punched the girl in the face, grabbed her by the hair and put her heel in the woman's neck.

"Let this be a lesson to you and I want you to tell all your friends or wanna be side chicks. This man belongs to me and only me. If you ever try to come at him again, your family will find your body floating in a river. Do I make myself clear?" When she didn't answer Violet stick the heel part deeper in her neck.

"Do I make myself clear?"

"Yes." You heard the woman whisper.

"Well damn. I see she isn't playing any games when it comes to you Miguel. You got a live one on your hands." Tony from New York laughed out.

"Really Miguel? You can't control your wife?" Otis said. The guy whose chick was getting up off the floor said.

"Nah, she had that. There was no need for me to say anything. But get this. Keep your hoes in check and it won't happen again." I told him raising my glass.

"Bitch if you ever…" Before she finished the sentence, my wife was beating her ass again. This time, she snatched the gun out of one of the guys' waist and pointed it straight at her.

"You got ten seconds to get the fuck out of here."

"Oh shit. I think you better keep quiet before we have to get a clean up crew in here for your ass." Tony said laughing. He was always clowning.

"Shut your dumb ass up Tony. You always talking shit."

"I'm just saying. This is what happens when you bring these hoes to our dinners instead of your wife."

"Exactly Tony." Violet chimed in.

"Otis how you going to ask him to control his wife, when she sat right there an made it obvious that she wants to sleep with her husband? You know damn well your wife would've down the same thing."

Otis didn't say anything. He handed the chick some more napkins to stop her nose from bleeding because I think V broke it. Those two left and we finished our dinner laughing and enjoying ourselves.

The other wives and Violet seemed to hit it off, well once everything died down. We were standing outside waiting for the driver when Tony walked up with his wife.

"Leave it to Otis to bring some trick here."

"I know but I'm sure we won't be seeing her anymore." I told him laughing.

"V. It was a pleasure seeing you again. I had a good time."

"Thanks Tony. I enjoyed myself as well." Her phone went off and she stepped away to answer it while I finished talking. My wife is definitely a force to be reckoned with.

Violet

The bitch straight disrespected me at dinner, so I had to show her my true colors. I didn't wanna fight but I was letting bitches know not to come for my man or me. In this day and age, these so-called side chicks don't care who they fuck. Especially, if they think it's going to make them a star. Fuck that. I'm not allowing any bitch to take what's mine. We worked too hard to stay together.

"Miguel can you pass me a Percocet?"

"Here baby. You know your arm isn't 100% yet."

"Sorry but she asked for that beat down. Both of them." He laughed shaking his head.

"You know I love you right." He said pulling me closer.

"Shit you better. I'm not out here whooping ass for nothing."

"Come on. I ran a bath for you. Then I have a masseuse coming to give you a massage. Maybe it will take the edge off your arm."

"Oooh is it a man." I joked.

"Yea a'ight V. Don't make me fuck you up."

"Awww you're jealous."

"Never that. No man can do what I do for you." I grinned because in all my years of living, the affect he had on my body was like no other.

The following day, Dom sent me a text message asking to meet up at some restaurant in Jersey City. Miguel was scheduled for another meeting and wouldn't be back until later, so I agreed.

"I'll be back later V."

"Ok baby. I'll be waiting for you." I closed the door behind him and went to get dressed.

I threw on some black skinny jeans with a white bustier crop top and a black blazer and the new black Beatrix Giuseppe's heels. My hair was straight already, I put on some lipstick and walked out feeling like a million bucks. I wanted to show him what he's missing and that my man is treating me well too.

Don't get it twisted. I can buy my own stuff, but Miguel's money is way longer then mine. Plus, half of the designers love him and send us the hot shit before it comes out. I put on my Prada shades and stepped in the truck. The ride was about forty minutes from the hotel we were at.

When I pulled up, the driver gave me an uncomfortable look. I know it's because we were in unfamiliar territory and no one was there to check the restaurant.

"Don't worry. No one knows I'm here; it'll be fine." I said trying to reassure him. I sent a message to Mariah telling her where I was and who I was with, just in case some shit popped off. I glanced around and spotted Dom in the corner waving me over. He stood up to give me a hug.

"Damn Violet. You're looking real, real good." He said trying to hug me. I pushed him back because I wouldn't disrespect my man like that.

"My bad." He looked offended and I didn't care. The waitress came over and I ordered a soda.

"What's up Dom? Why did you want to meet up? I thought I asked you not to contact me anymore."

"I miss you Violet and I know I fucked up by telling you to go on with your life."

"Dom, its too late for regrets now."

"You're right but you got a nigga ready to kill for you just to have you back." He said and continued undressing me with his eyes.

"I appreciate that but what's the real reason you called me here?"

"Violet, I have some important information that needed to be discussed face to face and not over the phone." I lifted my eyebrow at him.

"Dom, listen. What we had is over. I am a happily married woman and there's nothing you can say to me that will make me disrespect my husband. I can see this was a mistake to meet up with you."

"Violet, I wanted to ask if there were a way you could hook me up with your husband?" I looked at him like he was crazy.

"Hook you up with my husband for what?" I was hoping he wasn't about to say what I thought he was.

"You know. I just got out of jail and I need to get back on."

"What does that have to do with my husband?"

"Don't play games with me; I know your husband Miguel Rodriguez is the connect. He's supplying just about everyone in this country and others." I smirked and shook my head.

"My husband is a respectable business man who makes an honest living. For you to even assume he's involved in any drug activity is preposterous."

"Violet, don't be like that. We go way back and it's the least you could do, being as though I'm the only one who knows your secrets." He gave this sinister grin that sent chills through my body.

"After all these years Dom, you come to me and try to tell me my husband is dealing drugs and you're holding secrets only you and I share. If I didn't know any better, I would think this was a setup." I stirred the straw around my soda.

"Oh shit. What the fuck Violet? Did you call him?" I grinned. I didn't even need to turn around to know my husband was coming.

"Hey baby." He said kissing me before him; Ricardo and Hazel took a seat next to us. I told Hazel about the meeting with Dom this morning. I sent her a message to let her know what was going on; I knew she would bring him.

"What's up Dominic; is it?" Dom looked like he was about to shit on himself. He nodded to Ricardo who stood him up and patted him down. Sure enough, this nigga was wearing a wire.

"You've been in the game too long to know snitches aren't tolerated." Hazel said before pistol-whipping his ass. Thank goodness the restaurant was owned by one of Miguel's business associates and it was a slow day.

The area we were in, you couldn't see unless you came over there. I threw my soda in his face to wake him up.

"I know my wife asked you not to contact her anymore but for some reason you didn't listen and here we are. Did you really think she would snitch on her husband or better yet, allow you to hug or get her back?" His eyes popped open.

"Yea, those same detectives you made a deal with to get out of jail early with, are on my payroll." I gave my husband a crazy look. I had no idea he was setting my ex up.

"See, I wanted you to work for me because I heard so many good things about you before you went in. Unfortunately, you failed miserably, and you know what happens to people who do."

"Baby, you want to do it?" I took the gun out his hand and screwed on the silencer.

"Dom, I may have asked him to help you if you went about it the right way. But you're right about one thing."

"What's that?" He said trying to sound tough.

"You and I are the only ones who know my secrets; well my husband knows now, but it goes with you." I pointed the gun at him

"Wait Violet. Before you kill me there are two things I need to say."

"What?"

"Someone put a hit out on you." Miguel has his hand around his throat.

"Baby wait. If you kill him, we can't get any information from him." He moved his hands.

"Who put a hit out on her and why?" I heard Hazel ask.

"All I know is two people are working together. The guy is from here in the states and I don't know where the other person is from." He said.

"What's the second thing?" I asked.

"I really do still love you."

Phew! His head splattered across the back wall.

Miguel made a call for someone to clean up and within minutes the restaurant was closed down. Hazel told everyone she would pay for their meals. Once the guy came to clean up the place we headed back to the hotel.

"You know I'm not feeling this shit V." Miguel barked in the car.

"What?"

"Don't what me. I asked you to stay away from him."

"I know but I wanted to know what was so important, he kept contacting me after I told him not too."

"What did I tell you?" I didn't say anything.

"I already knew what he was up to and I didn't want him to drag you into it. He already tried with two others and failed but once you played into his trap, I couldn't allow him to live. Your past died when he did but that still doesn't erase the fact you could've walked into a trap. There were no bodyguards here; anything could've happened to you. Why don't you get that?"

"I'm sorry." I tried to kiss him and he turned his head. I really pissed him off because he never turned me away.

When we got back to the hotel. we packed and hopped on the jet to go home. He didn't speak to me the entire ride and when we got home, he didn't come in the room.

It was getting late and I was horny, and he wasn't giving me any dick. I stripped my clothes off and started thinking about him eating my pussy. My hands were rubbing my chest, then I placed one down to circle my clit. I stuck two fingers inside and whispered out his name. I felt my pearl getting hard.

"Fuck Miguel. I'm about to cum." My visions of him fucking me were so real, I came hard on my fingers.

"How was it?" My eyes popped open and he was standing there with his arms folded and a smirk on his face.

"Fuck you."

"Ugh, no it looks like you had enough for the night." He was being a smart ass.

"It was good. I don't need you."

"Yea ok. That finger action aint got shit on my dick." I saw him taking his clothes off.

"Whatever. It worked fine."

"Yea, but I bet it didn't feel the same."

"Goodnight Miguel." I went in the bathroom to take another shower. He stepped in when I got out. I threw on some lotion, a t-shirt and got in the bed. This nigga came out but ass naked and got in the bed. I knew his ass was being fucking smart, but I had a trick for his ass.

"Goodnight V." This motherfucker pulled me close like his dick wasn't poking me in the ass.

Miguel

Violet pissed me off that she went behind my back and went to see the nigga Dom after I asked her not too. I know she thinks she's tough but dealing with someone like me, enemies came from any and everywhere. We all have enemies no matter who we are, and I don't have any who want her dead. Now that we found out a hit was put on her she's about to be on lockdown. There's no way in hell I'm letting anyone take her from my kids or me.

The night we came back, she was mad because she was horny and I refused to give her any. I went to take a shower and she was pleasuring herself. The shit was so sexy and my dick was rock hard but I wasn't fucking with her. The way she came after saying my name, almost had me slip up but I caught myself. Now here it's been a month and I'm still being stingy with my dick.

"V it's time to go see the new house." I woke her up.

"Miguel, it's not done yet. Why am I going over there?"

"V, you asked to be a part of the building aspect so let's go. You wanted it built a certain way and the foundation part is up. The architect will be there so you can run all your ideas by him."

"All right damn." She pouted.

"You ok babe?" I was being smart because I know she was horny just like me. We fuck like rabbits and its been a minute.

"Yea why?"

"Oh, I thought you were cranky because you needed to feel me inside you."

"Ughhh, you make me sick. Keep playing with me. I'll fuck around and rape your ass." She laughed walking in the bathroom. I shook my head and got the kids ready with Karen.

"Why you dressed like that?" I asked her. She had on some tight ass jeans that had her ass looking fat. The shirt didn't cover her stomach and she had on some fuck me heels.

"Miguel there's nothing wrong with what I have on." She said smirking. I knew she was trying to get a rise out of me.

The day flew by and each time V walked in front of me, she would make sure her ass touched my dick. She was bending over in front of me pretending to pick shit up, but the best part was when she asked me to help her take her shirt off. She must've already taken the bra off because her tities popped right out. My mouth watered and I licked my lips as soon as I saw them.

I almost gave in but I was still going to try and hold out. I put the kids to bed, locked the doors and set the alarms. V was coming out the shower wrapped in a towel and I went in and shut the door. My dick was brick hard but I refused to get myself off so I turned on a cold shower. I came out and V was on the bed pouring chocolate syrup down her body and sucking on her finger; then placed it inside her.

"What the fuck V? This is some bullshit." I tried to walk past her but she stood in front of me and stuck her fingers in my mouth. It had been so long since I had a taste of her, I sucked on it for dear life.

"Mmmmm, that's some good stuff V." She placed my hand on her pussy and her tongue found mine.

"Nah V. I'm good." I pushed myself away from her. My dick was poking her in the stomach. She sat back on the dresser and cocked her legs open.

"Come here and get your pussy Miguel before I give it to someone else." When she said those words, I had my hand around her throat so quick I shocked both of us.

"Baby I'm sorry." I said in her ear. I felt a tear fall on my neck and when I glanced at her, she looked scared to death.

"V you know I didn't mean that." She pushed me out the way and went in the bathroom. I heard the shower start.

"FUCK!!!" I said out loud to myself. I stepped in the bathroom and she was on the shower floor in a zone again.

"Shit V. I'm sorry." I refuse to give her one of those pills. I didn't want her to get addicted to them. I sat behind her in the shower and just hugged her. I rubbed her hair and cradled her like she was my son or daughter. A few minutes later, she snapped out of it.

"Miguel, can you wash me up?" It was like she didn't even know what happened.

I had her stand and washed both of us up, carried her in the room to lie down but it was chocolate syrup on the bed. I ran to the closet and got a new set of sheets for the bed. After I made the bed, I laid her in it. I felt so fucked up, I had her lay under me all night.

The next morning, I had the kids bring her breakfast in bed. She smiled and kissed all three of us. I don't know if she didn't remember or just didn't want to talk about it but I had to go handle some business and I didn't wanna leave her. I really needed Hazel and Ricardo with me, so I asked my mom to come sit with her. She was the only person I trusted to be around her and my kids anyway.

"YOU DID WHAT?" My mom yelled at me in the living room when I explained what happened, minus V being naked. I told her we were playing, and she said it.

"I know ma. I wasn't thinking."

"Miguel, Violet is tough out in the streets but at home she's not when it comes to you and the kids. Ever since the accident, the shooting and now someone trying to kill her, she is so fragile. She's trying to put up a front and be strong for you because she doesn't want you to see her as a weak woman."

"I would never look at her like that. I know the crazy shit she did in her past and she's been doing a lot of crazy shit lately too. I know she has it in her so if she wanted to take a step back, I wouldn't be mad. I know she's a ride or die chick, but I need her to be my wife right now."

"Have you told her?"

"No because I didn't know it was this serious."

"Listen, go ahead and do what you need to. She'll be fine." My mom patted me on the shoulder.

"Ma, please take care of her. I'll be home as soon as I can."

"Miguel your wife will be fine and so will these bad ass kids." Jr. was throwing his trucks across the room and Joy was laughing at him.

"Don't talk about my babies." I gave all of them a kiss and went to check on my wife. She was lying in the bed watching TV.

"I'm going now V. My mom is here to help. If you need anything just holla."

"Baby, I'm ok. You didn't need to have your mom over." She sat up.

"I know but after last night, I wanted you to rest."

"Miguel, about that. I'm sorry you had to witness that again."

"You're my wife V. Whatever you go through, I'm going to be here to help you. Don't ever apologize and I wanna apologize for putting my hands around your neck."

"No, I should've never said it, even though I was playing. I would never let another man touch me."

"I know V but I still should've ever done that. To even think a man touched you, sent me over the edge."

"I love you baby." She said and kissed my lips.

"Are you going to leave me?"

"No silly. Please don't do it again. You scared me. The look in your eyes was like you were looking at someone else."

"I'm sorry Violet. I promise to never ever do it again."

"I believe you baby. Have a good day and be safe." I kissed her and walked out the room.

The day seemed to be dragging and I didn't know if it was because the shit with V was weighing heavy on me or because I just found out my cousin's girlfriend disappeared, and I needed to go to Jersey. I didn't want to leave V, but I wasn't sure if I should take her with me either.

"Hey you. I was just thinking about you." Violet said when she answered the phone.

"Oh yea. What about?"

"Ummm, the architect said we could have a passage way built behind the walls connecting each room. What do you think? I mean if anyone ever broke in the house it would be a good hiding place."

"I'm ok with whatever you want to have him do. I never question anything you when it comes to building your dream house."

"Oh stop. I want your input. That's why I'm asking."

"It's whatever you want." I told her again.

"Miguel, this is our dream house."

112

"Ugh, no. You made me sell my dream house."

"Boy, you know I was not moving in there with my babies where that slut bag whore was at." I laughed so hard on the phone she had to yell at me to stop.

"Ok, ok V. That's some shit Nino Brown said on New Jack City."

"I know that's where I got it from." We stayed on the phone a little longer. She was about to feed the kids and I told her I would be home later.

I was coming out the bathroom in my office drying my hands when I saw Faith sitting in the lobby.

"Mr. Rodriguez, Ms. Faith would like to speak to you. She claims she won't leave until you see her." My secretary said into the speaker. I blew my breath out and told him to allow her to come up.

When she stepped in my office she had on a short skirt, her blouse was extremely tight and basically, had her cleavage hanging out. I looked down at my wedding band and reminded myself of what I had at home. Was she worth losing my family over; I think not?

"What you want Faith?" I said in a harsh tone.

"Is that anyway to treat the woman you spent over ten years with?" She walked around my office.

"Faith, say what you need to say and bounce."

She sat on the edge of my desk with her legs open to show me she had no panties on. I glanced at my son and daughters' picture on my desk and scooted her off. I'm not going to lie and say she had me nervous, but the more I looked at my family, the easier it was to push her away. She took her hands and started rubbing in between her legs.

"Faith get the fuck out yo." I could see she was shocked. I usually fell for her shit but I was determined to stay faithful to my wife. I wouldn't put V through the same mess my dad put my mom through with mistresses all over the world.

The hurt and pain I saw was more then enough to know I could never do that to my wife. If I chose to be married it was forever and that's what V and I were.

"Miguel, you know you miss this." She unbuttoned her shirt and stepped outta the skirt. I went to hand her the clothes to put back on, when I felt a sharp pain in my side. I put my hand there and saw blood on my hand.

"Bitch what the hell?" I saw the grin on her face as she jabbed me again with something looking like a hunter's knife. She pushed it so deep the second time, that it broke off in my side.

"Miguel, I'm sorry but if I can't have you, neither will she." She rushed to put her clothes.

"Now since I was in your will to get the house you bought me, the ten million dollars and two vacation spots you inherited from your dad but didn't want, I think its time to cash in on them. I may not get all your money but ten million will do just fine."

"Are you fucking serious?" I could feel myself going in and out of consciousness. The blood was pouring out my side as I tried to apply pressure. She stood there waiting for me to die. Little did her dumb ass know, I been changed the will before Violet even came in the picture. If I died, she wasn't getting shit; the house I bought her was sold and the cars, I donated to charity.

"Hurry up and die Miguel damn. What the fuck?" She stood there tapping her feet. I could see my sister and Ricardo on my security cameras getting out their car to come back in. She must've noticed it too because she jumped off my desk.

"I really did love you Miguel. I'm sorry to see you go but I'll think of you with every dollar I spend." This bitch kissed me and hauled ass out the back door of my office. I showed her that in case of an emergency, now I regretted it.

I tried to get up to reach my door but I fell. I heard voices outside the office, but it seemed like they were taking forever to get to me. I saw flashbacks of me growing up, Violet having my son, us on our honeymoon and the last conversation she and I just had.

Next thing I know, I felt my body being lifted and I heard someone asking where the knife was. I don't know what happened afterwards because I fell asleep.

Hazel

Yesterday, Miguel and I had a meeting with some distributors from Brazil who wanted him to be his new connect. He wasn't happy with his current supplier and heard about my brother. We did an extensive background check on him and found out he was supplying tons of people out there but whoever his connect was, started cheating him out of drugs. The prices went up, the product wasn't good and the people weren't buying; which meant he was losing money.

Miguel never wanted anyone to see his face, so he always had someone else go in his place and pretend to be him. He sent Butch and a few other trusted men on his team over to Brazil to observe the drug game. Miguel still wanted his own law enforcement he could trust. He made sure each one he chose; were aware of everything they'd lose if they ever fucked up or decided to try and take him down.

Today we had a phone conference with any and everyone on his team. We sat there and listened to my brother be the boss he is.

"I decided to do business with you but here are the rule and consequences when working with me." The man stayed silent.

"The money is always due up front and the product will be delivered, an hour after. The drop-off will never be in the same spot and if something comes up where it needs to be change, you will be notified. The last thing I want your team to know is, I have information on each and every person and any fuck ups will be taken out on them and their families. I don't tolerate disrespect from anyone. Does everyone understand?" I heard yes's throughout over the phone, but I hate that I couldn't see. There was always a motherfucker waiting in the background to take the spot of the leader. I'm sure he would show his colors sooner or later.

After he hung the phone up, Ricardo and I decided to go out for lunch. Miguel didn't wanna go so we told him we'd bring him something back.

We got back from lunch and I thought I saw Faith's car in the parking garage. I walked up to it and sure enough it was hers. I could tell by the two garbage bags of clothes she still

had inside I handed her the night we put her out my brothers'
house.

"Ricky, Faith is here." He shook his head. He hated her
as much as I did. We pressed the elevator and stepped on.

Miguel owned the building and sub leased it out to
other companies, but our office was on the tenth floor. We
didn't need one, but he said he needed a place to conduct
meetings at. He owned so many businesses, I guess it made
sense to have an office instead of having people coming to his
house.

The eighth floor was human resources for the
businesses. That's where the hiring, orientation and firing were
done. The ninth floor was payroll and accounting and we had
the tenth floor to ourselves with a two big ass conference
rooms. It wasn't uncommon for us to have meetings on the
same day so two were necessary.

"Hazel, I'm about to take your brother his food and see
what the hell she's doing in there."

"Ok, I'm going to check my emails and return these
calls Alyssa handed me." She was my secretary and I loved her.

She was a ditzy white girl but her office skills were on point. Her dad was the Sergeant of the police department and that helped too. Him and Miguel played golf together sometimes.

Now Miguel's secretary was a guy Faith hired. She didn't want any females working under him and he could care less about shit like that, so he let her have her way. I took my heels off and slid my slipper Uggz on.

"YO, WHAT THE FUCK? CALL 911." I heard my husband yelled out.

I ran out my office and looked at Alyssa who jumped up running behind me. Bobby was on the phone dialing 911 like he was told.

I pushed open Miguel's door and saw him on the ground bleeding to death. I dropped and cradled him in my lap. Ricardo went running down the back steps to see if he could catch whoever did it.

"Mickey stay awake."

"I'm trying Hazel." He said weakly. The blood seemed to be pouring out of his side.

"Who did this?" He wouldn't answer but I know he heard me.

"Call Violet." He said before he closed his eyes.

"Mickey wake up. Don't go to sleep. Stay awake. Look I'm calling Violet. Your son is gonna wanna talk to you." He tried to crack a smile.

I heard the elevator doors open and EMT's rushed over to where he was. They slid that yellow board underneath him, then lifted him on the stretcher. They ripped his shirt off and applied pressure to one wound.

"Oh my God. What's the metal piece in his side?"

"Ma'am it looks like whatever he was stabbed with is still inside. We need to get him to a hospital and get it out. I need you to back up so I can start and IV." Alyssa grabbed my purse, cell and shoes and told me she would lock up. I trusted her because she's done it so many times.

Ricardo came back up and turned everything off in his office before locking the door. He drove behind the EMT while I drove in the back with Miguel. I could barely hold the phone in my hand as I tried to dial Violet's number. She didn't answer and neither did my mom, which had me worried.

"Ma'am he needs emergency surgery. Who are you to him?" The doctor asked.

"I'm his sister."

"Ok, I will keep you updated."

"I'll be right here. I'm waiting on his wife now." He nodded his head and the doors closed behind him. I went to call Violet again, but she was calling me.

"Hey Hazel. I'm sorry. We were outside with the kids and left the phone in the house. What's up?" I couldn't stop crying; Ricardo took the phone from me.

"Hey Violet."

"What's going on Ricardo?" I could hear her asking him on the phone.

"Violet leave the kids at the house with Karen and get to the hospital."

"I'm on my way. Is Hazel ok?"

"Yes, she's fine. It's Miguel; he was stabbed a couple times." I saw Ricardo look at the phone.

"She hung up on me."

"Maybe we should've have told her until she got here. You know how she is over him." He said making sense.

Violet and my mom came flying through the doors twenty minutes later.

"Who did this?" My mom asked as Violet sat in the chair next to me crying her eyes out.

"We don't know. Ricky found him like that. The last person in there with him was Faith. Mickey didn't say she did it, but I think she did."

"What was she doing in his office?" Violet wanted to know.

"I don't know. She wasn't in there long because she signed in the office around 1:15 and we got back at 1:30. We have no idea how long he was lying there."

We stayed there for hours waiting and the doctor finally came out. He told us my brother would be fine and the blade broke off in his side puncturing his lung.

He had two wounds; one required five stitches but the other one needed forty-five of them. The doctor also said he was very lucky infection didn't set in because that would have

been another problem. We thanked him and waited to go see

him.

Violet

Miguel's mom and I took the kids outside in the back to play and ended up out there longer than expected. We left our phones inside because we didn't think anyone would call.

I came in to get something to drink and grabbed my phone too. I went outside and called Hazel, who called five times back to back. When she told me, my husband was stabbed, the phone fell out my hand and disconnected.

"What's the matter Violet?" I felt my hands shaking.

"Miguel is in the hospital somebody stabbed him." I stood there in shock. I could hear his mom calling my name, but my body was frozen.

Karen helped bring the kids inside and his mom helped me in the car. She drove to the hospital because I couldn't. I walked in and saw the blood on his sister and the tears flooded my eyes even more than before. After the doctor came out and said he was ok and going to a room, I couldn't wait to see him.

He was asleep when they brought him in due to the anesthesia and pain medication. I sent Hazel and Ricardo home and his mom went to my house. I told them it was no sense in them sitting up there knowing he'll probably sleep all night. The nurses brought me some sheets and blankets. They had a chair in there with cushions that turned into a bed when you pulled it open.

I laid there watching him breath in and out, scared to go to sleep. My anxiety was at an all time high and it was taking everything in me to stay calm.

"Violet." I heard him whisper out. I sat up in the chair and went to his side.

"Yea baby. I'm here. How are you feeling?" I asked pressing the call button for the nurse.

"I'm ok." He wiped the tears from my eyes and placed his hand on my stomach.

"I knew it."

"Yea you called it baby. The first appointment is in two weeks, so you have to get better.

"I'm going to be fine by then."

"I know you are."

"V." He called out to me again.

"Yea Miguel."

"Do you know I could've died, and you would've never had any more of this dick or my tongue." I bust out laughing.

"That's ok. I would've stayed celibate, used my fingers and memories just to keep the last feeling we had."

"I love you Violet."

"I love you too." The doctor and nurse came in explaining to him what they did. Not too long after, he drifted back to sleep.

The next few days were tough because he wanted to get back to work and the doctor said he couldn't. The day he was released, I had a male nurse come over the first night to show me how to change his dressing.

Day after day Miguel started getting his strength back. The doctors' appointment came and went. He told us we were six weeks pregnant and that he sees us every few months. It was funny but he was telling the truth.

"Are you going to tell me who did this to you?" I asked my husband when we went out to eat.

"V, I don't want to talk about it right now. We're celebrating me putting another athlete in you." I knew he was avoiding the question, so I let it be for now.

He and I went to the mall and brought a bunch of shit neither one of us needed. When we got home there was a box on the front porch addressed to me.

"Don't open it until I get someone to check that shit."

"Stop it Miguel. No one knows where we live." I took it in the house and left it on the counter because the kids came running up to us. We played with the kids all day and after dinner watched a movie. The kids didn't go to bed until late, which meant they would sleep in.

"Miguel can you unsnap this for me?" It was a necklace I couldn't undo because of my nails. He laid it on the dresser and stood behind me staring at us in the mirror. He slid my hair to the side and trailed kisses down my neck while rubbing my breast from behind.

"Mmmmm." I moaned out.

"How does it feel V?" I couldn't speak with his fingers flickering my pearl. He spun me around to face him, sat me on the dresser and rammed himself inside. The impact was a bit painful but the pleasure that followed, was worth it.

"V, this pussy is always the best."

"Is this dick mine?" I asked throwing my pussy back at him.

"Yes baby. This dick will always be yours. Shit, Fuck." I felt his dick twitching inside me.

"Oh no. You're not about to cum. I've waited over a month for this. You better hold it in." He laughed and lifted me up off the dresser, still inside me. He gently laid me on the bed and spread my legs far apart and dug deeper.

"Oh my God, I'm cumming baby." I pushed his dick out with my juices and flipped him over to get on top.

"V, you know I'm going to cum like this." I was in a zone and couldn't hear shit he was saying. That spanish started coming out of him and there was no turning back. I stood on my feet and dropped my pussy on his dick harder and faster, over and over.

"Aw shit V. Here I cum girl. Don't stop baby. Make daddy cum."

"Cum for me daddy. Shit, I'm cumming with you."

"Awwww Fuckkkkk Violet." He came so much inside me, I felt his dick thumping like he couldn't stop. I moved down and sucked him off like this was my last time tasting him.

"V what are you doing to me?" His hands were on my head but when he was about to cum, he stopped me and made me get up.

"Fuck this shit. Turn around and assume the position." I got on all fours, felt him spread my ass cheeks and legs wider while he gave me the best pussy assault I had in my life with his dick. I couldn't stop myself from cumming.

"Miguel, I love you so much baby. Please stop. I can't cum any more." He continued until I felt him grunting.

"I swear if you ever give this pussy away, I'm killing you and him. Shit, baby here I cum." I jumped off and sucked him dry.

"Ahhh Violet, suck all of it."

"Mmmmm."

"Yea girl just like that. Fuck you have the best pussy in the world hands down. Bring that ass up here and give me a kiss." He said trying to catch his breath.

"You have the best dick in the world and if you give it out to anyone, I'm cutting it the fuck off, then killing you." He chuckled but he better know I wasn't playing.

"V, I'm not messing up anything for you to leave me. The love I have for you is growing deeper everyday and the way we just fucked each other, let me know no other woman can do me like you."

"Good."

"Trust me. I've had my share of women and none of them can compare to what you have in between your legs or what your mouth can do." He told me in between kisses.

"Bring that pussy up here so I can taste it before I go to sleep."

"I don't think I can cum anymore. How about I give it to you for breakfast?" He sat up on his elbows and I could feel him looking down on me.

I was lying on my stomach when he pulled my legs to the edge of the bed and pushed my ass up just enough for him to stick his face inside and open up the floodgates in my pussy again. I came so much tonight, there was no way I had any fluids left in my body. I made him get me two bottles of water out the fridge when he was finished.

****

Over the next few months he and I had been back and forth to the new house and we were moving in this weekend. Everything was packed and the movers were coming in two days. We weren't taking much because all the furniture was new.

He and I had just finished making love again like we did almost every night; except a few times he stayed at the office late.

He was in the shower when I looked down and noticed his phone going off. I didn't feel the need to look so I left it. It rang a few times again, but the number was blocked.

"Hello." I answered thinking nothing of it.

"Can I speak to Miguel?" Some female asked in the phone.

"I'm his wife. Can I ask why you're calling him so late and what's this about?"

"I know it's his wife, and?" She started getting smart on the phone.

"If you know about me, then why are you calling?" I was getting pissed because not only was she rude but also being disrespectful.

"Just tell him I had a good time when he was here, and I wanted to know when he was coming back?"

"Ok dummy. First of all, once he finds out you told me about this little rendezvous you're claiming whatever you two had, will be over."

"That's what you think."

"No, it's what I know."

"Oh, I see you didn't open the little box I sent you."

"What box?"

"The one that should've been delivered weeks ago."

"Anyway, tell Miguel I miss his big ass dick and can't wait to feel him inside me again." She hung the phone up and I heard the shower go off. I jumped out of bed and threw my robe on.

"Hey, I thought you were coming to shower with me."

"I was but your phone kept going off." He looked over at the nightstand where it was and I saw it started ringing again from the same number. I knew it was the bitch hoping he would answer it. That's what bitches do after they speak to the wife; continue to call, hoping he would answer after she kicked him out, but I had a trick for her ass.

"Answer it baby." I stood there with my arms folded. I didn't wanna forget about the box so when he walked to pick it up, I ran to get it out the closet where I left it. I figured it was a new gadget I ordered for the kitchen since I stayed watching QVC and ordering shit. I came back in and was flabbergasted by his conversation.

"Are you fucking crazy calling my phone? What if my wife answered?" I could tell at that moment she told him I already did.

He turned around and looked straight in my face. I started opening the box and what I saw next had me disgusted. Here I was four months pregnant, glaring at pictures of my husband's dick in some chick's mouth. There were a few of him fucking her from behind and the ultimate disrespect was the picture of him in between her legs. He disconnected the call and walked towards me.

"Don't even think about touching me." I sat on the bed with my head down as he stood in front of me.

"V, let me explain."

"Nope." I shook my head wiping the tears.

"Do you love her?"

"I don't know." I looked up and he was leaning against the dresser.

"Huh? You don't know? What kind of shit is that?"

"I said, I don't know."

"Nah nigga. Either you do or you don't, there's no fucking in between."

"I don't want to talk about this anymore." He said putting his wife beater on and getting in the bed.

"Oh ok. Well then, let's not." I went into the kitchen and grabbed the biggest butcher knife I could, went in the room with my hand behind my back. He looked at me like I was crazy.

"V come get in the bed. I'm tired and you know I can't sleep without you." I laughed at his dumb ass if he thought this shit was over.

I sat on the bed next to him and rubbed on his dick to get him hard. It didn't take long for him to wake up. His eyes were closed as he enjoyed the hand job I was giving him.

I grabbed his dick tightly and put the knife right at the base of his dick. He must've felt the coldness of it and pushed me off the bed before I could chop his shit off.

"Are you fucking crazy V?" My eyes were watering. I got off the floor and ran towards him again with it, but he grabbed my wrist.

"V, stop this shit." He got the knife from me and threw me on the bed. He tried to kiss me but I turned my face from him. When I felt his dick poking at my entrance, I kneed the hell out of him.

"I wish the fuck you would try and fuck me after I found out about you and your mistress. Get the fuck out." He was holding himself on the ground. I stood there watching his dumb ass get himself together after he recuperated from it.

He threw some clothes on and jumped in his car, but you bet a bitch was right behind him. After about thirty minutes he pulled up to the house I told him to get rid of and some bitch answered the door. I couldn't believe he had her right under my nose. I looked on my keychain to see if I still had the key and voila, I did.

It was easy for me to get in because there was no security or surveillance anywhere. I opened the door and heard some yelling upstairs in one of the bedrooms. I stood outside the door and listened.

"Why the fuck would you call my phone this late and tell my wife? Better yet when the fuck did you take those pictures?"

"Does it matter Miguel. Now we can be together. You kept saying you were going to leave her." I knew the voice, but I couldn't place it.

"Yo, I never told you I was leaving my wife. There's nothing you or any other woman can do to make me leave her."

"Then why are you cheating on her with me? Why did you move me out here? I mean what the fuck is up?" *He moved her out here? Who the fuck is this bitch?*

"Look, you said you didn't have anywhere to go so don't make it seem like I'm loving you. Second, you and I only fucked a few times and I told you to leave this house."

"Don't you love me baby?" She asked him and I couldn't wait to hear the answer.

"My wife asked me that same shit tonight."

"What did you tell her?"

"I told her I didn't know. But the longer I sit here with you, it couldn't be any clearer that I'm not. I swear if I lost her, I don't know what I'm going to do." I heard the pain in his voice, but it was too late; he lost me for sure.

"Come here let me make you feel better." I heard her unbuckling his pants.

"Nah, I'm good my wife gave me what I needed."

138

"Well then can you give me what I need?"

"And what is it that you need?" He said entertaining the shit.

"I need to feel that tongue again."

"Bitch, you crazy as hell."

"What? Don't act like you never did it."

"You got lucky one time. I was drunk and you kept talking shit about how you wanted me to pretend you were my wife. My dumb ass fell for it but you better believe you won't ever get that. My tongue better yet my mouth is for my wife only."

"How about we act like I'm her again?"

"How about not?" I said busting through the door. The shock on both of their faces was priceless but mine was worse when I saw who she was.

Miguel

When Violet burst through the door, I knew it was about to be World War 3. The look on my wife's face when she saw who the woman was, let me know I hurt her in the worse way. I didn't mean for us to hook up, but the bitch found me. I don't know how but she did, and I thought she wouldn't say anything because of their history. I guess I was wrong because here we are.

The night we came back from Jersey after Violet beat the woman up at the bar and the shit happened with her ex, I was sitting in my office at work.

"Mr. Rodriguez there's a Pamela Winston here to see you." I looked on the screen and I knew the woman but couldn't place her. She was very pretty, and her body was all that. You know the fat ass, big tities, no waist type of shape. I stepped out to get her and then it dawned on me who she was.

"What are you doing here and how did you find me?"

"Is that anyway to treat the lady who can have your wife arrested for assault and use of a deadly weapon?"

140

*"Bitch, please. You asked for that ass whooping, twice;
I may add when you disrespected her. Then you think you can
come in here and threaten me about filing charges against my
wife. You must look at me as a dumb nigga." I told her. This
bitch was so quick that her mouth was around my dick within
seconds. I know I should've stopped her but I was still mad at
V. I came all over the bitch face.*

*"Damn, that shit taste good. I wonder how you feel."
There was no way in hell I was fucking her. I escorted her
dumb ass out and told her not to come back.*

*Later on that night, I worked late because I was still
debating on working with the Brazilian dude. It was after
eleven and even my sister had gone home. I don't know how
the bitch got in but I came out my office getting ready to lock
up and she stepped off the elevator with two bottles of Patron.*

*I don't know why but I stayed a little longer drinking
with her and I could feel the effects of the liquor kicking in. She
was licking her lips and touching on herself in front of me.*

*"You got that earlier but there's no way I'm fucking
you." She went and locked the door to my office and pulled out*

141

a bag from Walgreens. Inside was a 3 pack of magnum condoms. This bitch came ready to fuck. She undressed herself and my dick grew at the site of all that ass.

I ripped open the pack of condoms, slid one on and turned her around. Her ass jiggled over and over causing me to cum quick. I didn't care. She didn't deserve a lot of my time anyway. She laid back on the floor with her legs cocked open like I was supposed to eat her pussy.

"Nah, I don't do that."

"Come on. You know you want to."

"No I don't. Only for my wife."

"Then pretend I'm your wife. Come on Papi, suck this pussy." When she said Papi, I heard Violet's voice because that's what she calls me. It had to be the liquor, but I had the bitch screaming my name and running from my tongue.

After I made her cum a few times, I put another condom on and fucked the shit out of her. She got on top and rode my dick the way I liked it. I felt the condom pop and I kindly removed her off of me and put the other one on. No other woman was having my kids but my wife.

"Damn Miguel this dick is all that. No wonder she didn't want me having it. Fuck, I'm about to cum."

"Cum for me then." When she let it out, this bitch howled, and her body jerked a few times.

I helped her up and both of us took turns washing up in the bathroom. I wasn't going home smelling like another woman.

V was asleep when I got home which was a good thing. The next few weeks, I would fuck Pam at least two or three times a week. She didn't drain me like V did, so if my wife wanted to have sex, I was still able to do it.

One day she told me it was time for her to go back to the states, and she didn't have anywhere to stay so I offered her the old house I had. V told me to get rid of it but I had yet to put it on the market and she's been here for the last two months.

The day I got stabbed, I vowed to never cheat on my wife again. I gave Pam whatever she wanted as far as money, a car and told her she could stay in the house until further notice but she fucked up when she told V and now I'm sitting her trying to diffuse a situation that's about to end up badly for

Pam.

"So, I guess you didn't take heed to my warning when I almost killed your ass back in the states huh?"

"V calm down."

"Bitch, I guess he wasn't your man as much as you thought he was; now was he?"

"Pam don't antagonize her."

"Nah, she's right Miguel. You're just out here slinging your dick from ho to ho. Why did I beat her ass for the licking her lips gesture when you were just going to fuck her anyway?"

"Violet it wasn't like that. She came to me talking about pressing charges on you and then one thing led to another. I'm not going into detail because that's irrelevant."

"Ok, so you allowed this trick to threaten me and you fell for it knowing who you are?"

"The problem with the wives is they think their pussy is golden and their men won't cheat, but you see its women like us. What did you call me a side bitch right? I'm right there to give your man what he needs, when he needs it."

"See, and the problem with you side bitches are the husbands you're cheating with, doesn't and won't ever love you. He looks at you like a piece of ass he can have whenever he wants but know this. This man right here, this husband, can have your ass because the one thing I don't do is fuck after trash. And that's exactly what you are."

"Violet, I'm not going anywhere, and neither are you." She had this evil look on her face and for a moment she had a nigga nervous.

"Yea Violet. Let me finish with him tonight and I promise to send him back home before the kids wake up." That was it. Violet beat the shit out of her.

"It doesn't matter how many times you fight me, I'm still going to fuck him." Pam kept antagonizing her.

"Shut the fuck up Pam. You're making the shit worse."

"Fuck that bitch Miguel. Does she know about the car you brought me and all the clothes? Don't forget the money I get from you weekly." She said laughing with blood coming

145

from her mouth. The look on my wife's face said it all. I couldn't deny shit as she took off examining the closet. There was so much shit in there. It was like a store.

"Violet let me talk to you."

"No need. She said enough. I'll see you when you get home or are you staying out tonight?" I gave her the side eye.

"You know I'm not staying here."

"Ok, I'll see you soon then. Bye." She went down the steps and left. I wanted to smack the shit out of this stupid bitch. She was in the bathroom rinsing her mouth out and looking at the bruises V left on her.

I wasn't sure I should go home so I went to my moms' house and slept in the guest bedroom. The next day, I heard my mom yelling in the other room.

"Miguel. Miguel get up something happened to Violet." She screamed making me jump out the bed.

"What's the matter? What happened to her?"

"I don't know. Hazel said the nanny called and told her the EMT's took her to the hospital. What happened over there? Wait; why the fuck did you sleep here? What the fuck is going on?" I grabbed my keys and hopped in my car racing to the hospital.

"Slow the hell down Miguel." My mom yelled and popped me upside the head.

"Hi, my wife was brought in. Can you tell me if she's ok?" I gave the receptionist my wife's name. She told me the doctor would be out to speak with me soon. I saw this man in a suit come in asking for Violet, along with two officers who were on my payroll.

"Hey Mr. Rodriguez. What are you doing here?" The one cop asked. I told him my wife was brought in and asked him the same thing.

"Oh. I didn't know this was your wife. Look, I don't want any problems. I was told we needed to get to the hospital and stand guard while her lawyer went in to talk to her."

"Lawyer. What kind of lawyer?" When he said divorce lawyer, I lost it.

"Nah, you can tell that motherfucker to leave right now. Ain't nobody getting a divorce." My mom tried to calm me down, but it took Ricardo and the two cops to get me outside.

147

"Yo, calm down Miguel. I don't know what's going on but you can't be in here acting up like this. You're drawing too much attention to yourself." Ricardo said.

"I just wanna see my wife, that's all." We sat out in the lobby area for hours, when the lawyer came out and told us we can go back there now. The doctor never told us what happened so when we got to her room Hazel was helping her get dressed.

"What the fuck Violet?" I barked staring at her.

"Not right now Miguel." My sister said walking her out the room.

"What you mean not right now? Then when?"

"Let me get her home and then I'll come by mom's and explain everything to you." Violet wouldn't even look at me.

I went to my mom's house, took a shower and threw on clothes I had Ricardo drop off to me. It took Hazel three hours to come back to my mom's house, who was waiting herself to find out what happened. When Hazel walked in, she had a look of hate on her face.

"What Hazel?"

"Nothing. Nothing at all." He shook her head.

"Well what happened to her? Why was she in the hospital?" My mom asked.

"The shit you pulled last night sent Violet over the edge. She had a nervous breakdown and when Karen found her, she was on the floor naked with slits to both of her wrists. She said there was so much blood and Violet was barely breathing." I fell back on the couch. I didn't know what to say. I never thought I'd drive my wife to try and kill herself.

"Oh my God. Why did she do that? I'm surprised the hospital didn't admit her." My mom gasped and covered her mouth.

"The only reason they didn't is because she put me down for the next of kin and they knew I wouldn't allow it."

"Jesus, what about the baby?" My mom asked and Hazel looked at me.

"The baby is gone. The lack of oxygen from Violet being passed out caused her to miscarry. How could you Miguel?" I couldn't do shit but sit there in total disbelief.

"What did Miguel do?" There was a knock at the door and when my mom opened it; there stood Violet with the kids.

"Miguel, I'm going to my moms for a while. I need you to take the kids." She handed me some papers along with the kids and their things.

"What the fuck you mean? You're not going anywhere."

"Miguel please. You did this. This is all your fault." She started banging on my chest crying; making the kids upset. My mom took them to the back and came back out.

"Let me talk to you V." I grabbed her arm before she could walk away.

"No, go talk to Pam, Faith or whoever."

"Faith? Where did that come from?" She chuckled.

"Oh, she called me too and informed me that not only was she the one who stabbed you, but you had her in your will. Yea, she's still waiting on her money and the other shit you offered her."

"She's not in my will."

"Well she seems to think differently." She wiped her eyes.

"You know I asked who stabbed you and you refused to talk about it; now I see why."

"Violet." She put her hand up for me not to speak.

"I loved you unconditionally; even with all your flaws and you broke my heart. And to think, I wanted to beat Hazel to see if I would get to ten kids before her." She sucked her teeth.

"Damn, I was so blinded by you. I can't believe I allowed this shit to go on right under my nose. But hey you live, and you learn right? Goodbye Miguel."

"Nah, V you're not leaving me."

"It's for the best. Look at it this way Miguel. You can do you and not have to answer to anyone."

"That's not what I want Violet."

"It doesn't matter anymore Miguel. You wanted to be single and sleep with all these different women who wanted what you had to offer money wise. Poor little me, didn't want anything but you and you couldn't give it to me, so I'm gone. I'll be back in a couple of weeks. Take care of my babies."

"So you're just going to leave your kids? What kind of mother are you?" She snapped her head back.

"I'm the kind of mother who has cared for them, day in and day out. The kind of mother who stopped working to be a stay at home mom. The one who catered to their daddies every need, only to be made a fool of. You can take care of them for a couple of weeks. It won't kill you. Karen is going to be staying here with your mom if that's ok so she can help out."

"Well fuck you Violet. I don't need you."

"And now the real Miguel comes out. Go ahead. Degrade and disrespect me to make yourself feel better. I know it's what you do to make everything ok with how you treated me. Hazel, I'll call you when I land."

"You must be flying commercial because you're not taking my jet."

"Your jet." She laughed.

"Nigga, that's our jet. Any and everything you got, I own half of it. So if I want to take it I can. Luckily, I'm the bitch that don't need you. You can keep all your shit. I don't want any of it. Bye asshole." I went to run after her and Ricardo caught me.

"Let her go man."

"Nah, fuck that." I heard the car pull off and Ricardo let me go. I went in one of the rooms and slammed the door. This shit was crazy.

Hazel

When Karen called me about Violet, I was worried something happened to the baby and Miguel was out of town or something. I didn't know the extent of what went down until I got there and saw for myself. They had her in a private room with a guard standing outside her door for safety.

I walked in and she had bandages wrapped around both of her wrist and they were getting ready to take her to get a DNC done, due to the miscarriage. Before she went in, she asked me to call her a lawyer and have papers drawn up to file for a divorce. I didn't want to but she said, it was the only way.

I didn't call my mom right away because I knew she'd tell my brother. I made the call when she was awake from the DNC. It took my brother less than ten minutes to get to the hospital. I thought the lawyer would've gotten there sooner but he came behind Miguel.

"What did your brother do?" My mom asked handing me a cup of coffee. I leaned my head back to see if the door was still closed to the room he was in. I filled my mom in on what V told me and she was just as surprised as I.

"Mom, you had to see her in the hospital. It was like she was a different person. Miguel did a number on her and it's fucked up because he went to great lengths to get her, only to lose her." We heard the door open and he came walking out like he had an attitude.

"She isn't getting shit. I mean it." He sat back and opened the papers from the lawyer.

"Miguel do you hear how you sound? She was your wife."

"Exactly, was."

"Where did I go wrong with you? I never raised you to be disrespectful to women; better yet your wife. I thought after you saw everything your father put me through, you would want to do better. How could you bring that much pain to her after I told you how fragile she was when it came to you."

"Fuck her. She wants it to be over, let it be over. She still aint getting shit." I was pissed at him and the dumb shit he was saying.

"Nigga, if you read the paperwork she doesn't want anything from you. Not a damn dime. The lawyer asked her multiple times if she was sure she wanted to throw it all away and she told him yes. If she took anything from you then she would be tied to you with that too. She even signed you can share custody."

"She's not taking my kids."

"MIGUEL!" My mom yelled at him.

"What?"

"You're treating her like she was a jump-off or a side bitch. What has gotten into you?"

"Nothing, I'm good. I'll have my lawyer look over this and if it's all good, I'll sign them in the morning."

"Damn, you won't even fight for her."

"For what Hazel? Fight for what? You know I don't chase bitches. Never have, never will. If this is what she wants, and I don't have to give her shit, then she can have it. My kids won't be homeless and until she finds somewhere to live, they will stay with me or one of you."

"What about her dream house you let her have built." I asked.

"Are you crazy. You think I'm giving her a divorce and then she gets with another nigga and he'll be in there. Nah, you got me fucked up."

"I never thought I would see the day when you would treat your wife, the mother of your kids, like a piece of trash. Who would've thought you'd turn into daddy?" I told him. I grabbed my keys and walked out. He came running behind me just as my phone rang.

"Hello." I put her on speaker.

"Hazel, I just wanted to tell you I made it here safe. Also, when you get a chance, can you send me some houses for sale? I know he's not going to allow me to stay in the new house; not that I would want to anyway."

"V, you can stay with me or my mom until we find you a house. But yes, I'll send you my realtors' number and she can hook you up." He stood there smoking and staring in the sky.

"Oh, can you tell Miguel he needs to pay Karen because I'm not there and I forgot to leave her a check?"

"I'll pay her. Don't worry about it. How are you feeling?"

"I'm good. It's going to take some getting used to. I've been with him for a couple of years and right now I'm missing him like crazy. I want him to hug me and make love to me and say everything is going to be ok but it's not. I swear I feel like I'm dying inside without him, that's why I needed to get away. I swear I wasn't trying to leave my kids, but I can't deal right now." I saw a few tears roll down his face when she said it.

"I know V. It's going to hurt for a while but you're strong. Trust me. I know you'll get through it."

"Hazel, I just want to say thanks for being there for me every time I needed a friend, a sister and just someone to listen."

"Violet."

"What's up Hazel?" I could hear her sniffling in the background. I could tell she was crying.

"Just know I'll always be here for you and you'll always be my sister."

"Thanks girl. Let me get off this phone. Mariah is cursing me out because she wants me to go out with them this weekend and I keep saying no."

"Well if you go out be careful and I love you girl. I'll see you when you get back." I hung the phone up and I could tell how hurt my brother was because even though he wiped the tears, I saw his eyes were still glossy. I went to get in the car and he stopped me.

"Hazel, I need you to go to Jersey this weekend and watch over her."

"What do you mean watch over her? Dayquan and her other brothers are there. They won't allow anything to happen to her."

"Please Hazel." I could see desperation in his eyes.

"If you think I'm going to spy on her for you nigga, you bugging. You made this mess and now you wanna act like you're trying to protect her."

"Hazel, are you going to do it or not?"

"Fine. But I'm not giving you any information on what she does."

"I'll find that out with or without you I just need you to protect her just in case. No one knows about us and I would hate for some nigga to try her."

"Ugh, you mean you don't want her to meet someone else."

"Whatever. When are you leaving?"

"Dam, it's only Wednesday. I'll leave Friday morning." He kissed me on the cheek and thanked me.

****

Violet and Ang picked me up at the private airport and we went out to eat for lunch.

"I saw a few houses I really liked. Do you think you can check them out for me? I want to move into my own place sooner than later."

"Sure."

"I know you and your mom don't mind but I need to have my own spot. If I don't have to be around him, I don't want to." I saw a few tears escaping her face when she spoke him up.

Miguel: *Are you there yet?*

Me: *Yes.*

Miguel: *How is she?*

Me: *Still a mess. You ain't shit.*

Miguel: *Whatever. Just keep her safe.*

Me: *Bye asshole.*

The girls and I went out Friday and Saturday night. Violet seemed to be in her own world the entire time, but you could tell she was trying.

Sunday when she dropped me off at the airport, she gave me a letter to give my brother. I wanted to read it with my nosy ass but I didn't want to see any nasty freaky shit, so I didn't open it.

I stopped by the house he and V were at before the new house was built, and he was inside lying on the couch watching TV.

"What are you doing here? Why didn't you move into the new house?"

"I'm not moving in there. This place will do just fine." He started flipping through the channels.

"Well she's safe and I think she's finally getting herself back to normal." He sucked his teeth when I said that.

"Oh, she gave me this to give you."

He sat up on the couch and took the letter from me. I gave him a kiss on his cheek and left the house. I didn't want to be on the receiving end of whatever the letter said. I did what he asked me to do and it was time for me to go home and be with my own family.

I walked in my bedroom and found my husband and daughter asleep. I pray to God I never have to deal with the shit my brother took Violet through.

Violet

To my dearest Miguel,

I hope when you get this letter you are in the best of health. First off, I want to start off by saying I don't want to fight with you. I want us to be friends again one day but right now, we both need some time away from one another. I know you sent your sister to keep an eye on me, but I don't need your protection anymore. As long as the kids are protected it doesn't really matter what happens to me.

I'll be back in a couple of weeks and hopefully the papers are signed, and my house will be ready. Anytime you want to see the kids on the days I have them just shoot me a text and I can drop them off to your sister or mom.

I don't know what I did to make you cheat or disrespect me the way you did but I get it. You don't want to be tied down and there's too much temptation out there. I just wish you told me that before you kidnapped my heart and soul.

This heartbreak is extremely hard on me and I feel like I'm dying without you. I need you to tell me it's not over. I *need you to want me the way I want you, but I know that's not possible because right now it's all about you. You're the most powerful man in so many countries and to be tied down is not in your future. I just want you to know I will always love you and you'll always have a place in my heart.*

P.S. Whatever woman you decide to be with, make sure she is good to our kids and I will do the same if I meet someone. Take care Miguel. Love V.

I cried the entire time as I wrote the letter to him. I knew it would be hard getting over him, but this is too much for me. I could see the sadness everyone had for me but I knew it was just a matter of time before I was back to my old self.

I went out to the mall with Heaven when some guy approached me. He was brown skinned with some dreads to the middle of his back; he had a medium build and his swag had my attention.

"Hello sexy." He said grabbing my hand. Usually, I hate for a man to do that but because he was sexy himself, I let it go.

"Hello." Heaven stood there grinning. I know it was because she wanted me meet someone new.

He and I spoke for a few minutes and exchanged numbers. I told him I lived in Puerto Rico and here visiting. He said he had family there and was willing to travel.

I got back to my mom's house and the dude sent me a text asking to go out to dinner on Friday, which were a few days away. I agreed to at least get out the house.

Friday came too quick and I was still in the house with Mariah trying to decide what to wear. She told me to wear something decent just in case he wanted to go out afterwards. I put on a cream sweater dress with some thigh boots. Mariah put some pin curls in my hair and my makeup was flawless.

I got to the restaurant before him and let the waitress seat me. When he came in, I stood up and he licked his lips, which told me he approved of my outfit.

"Violet, I have to say you are beautiful." I blushed like a high school girl.

"Thanks. You look good yourself." He was wearing all black Khakis, a fitted white shirt and some Prada sneakers. We talked over dinner and our conversation flowed well. I looked at my phone that vibrated and it was a message from Miguel.

Miguel: *I got your letter a few days ago.*

And that was the end of the text. I didn't respond back because I didn't feel like it required one. I was happy he knew how I felt. Hopefully, when I went back next week, we could at least be cordial.

Jeremy and I drove to the club in separate cars but sat together in VIP. Some of his friends came in and I felt a bit uncomfortable by the way they stared. I stepped out on the dance floor when *Hold you down* came on by DJ Khaled. Jeremy joined me and we stayed out there dancing and grinding on one another.

I looked up into the face of that stupid nigga Otis who was at the dinner a few months back with the whore my husband was fucking. I saw his ass grinning and I swore he snapped a picture. He walked over to me because Jeremy walked away to talk to someone.

"What are you doing here without your husband? And looking good enough to eat I might add. And I mean that literally." He licked his lips and tried to kiss my neck.

"Whoa. What the fuck are you doing?" I asked pushing him off me.

"Nothing. I'm just trying to get to know you a little better. Our last encounter was not a good one. And since your husband is fucking my side chick, I don't see why we can't be friends."

"Whatever my husband is doing doesn't concern you. If you thought I didn't know about the whore next door, I'm fully aware." I told him.

"Oh, you're one of those women."

"One of what women?"

"The kind who will allow her man to walk over her and she stays, because of his money and power."

"Again, what my husband and I have going on doesn't concern you."

"Ok, well let me ask you this. Why are you out here allowing this nigga to touch and feel all over you, while your husband is in Puerto Rico fucking Pam? I guess y'all have an open relationship huh?"

"Otis, what is it you really want? I know you didn't come over here to discuss Miguel or why I'm dancing with someone else."

"I just want to know what you have in between your legs because that nigga going crazy over you."

"What are you talking about?"

"Before you walked in that night, he made sure to tell each and everyone of us privately if any of us got close to you we were dead on sight. I'm saying. Can I get a taste or what?" This motherfucker took his hand and started sliding it up my thigh. I looked around for Jeremy and he was nowhere in sight. Was that a coincidence? He started kissing on my neck and I knew it was now or never.

"Come on Otis." I grabbed my things, took his hand and headed for the bathroom. It was too crowded, so we stepped outside. I left something in the door so it wouldn't close all the way.

"Damn Violet, your skin is soft as hell." He was rubbing on my ass and trying to go up my dress. He wasn't even turning me on which made what I was about to do easier. I observed my surroundings and there were no cameras or even cars on this side of the building. It was nothing there but an open lot.

"What do you want from me Otis?" He didn't speak and shoved his tongue in my mouth.

"I wanna taste you." He slid his fingers up my dress and just that quick, I slit his throat from ear to ear and his blood squirted on my clothes. I sent Mitch a text saying, I needed him right away and he had to send the two guys from his clean up crew.

They were there in less than twenty minutes getting rid of the body. I drove his car home and gave him the keys to mine. No one could see me with all this blood on me.

"Bitch. Why the fuck you out here killing niggas and shit?" Mariah yelled when I walked in her house.

"I'm going back to P.R tomorrow. It's too much going on out here." I changed clothes and booked a flight leaving in a few hours.

"What the hell happened? And where was the dude you went with?" Just as she asked, he sent a message saying he was sorry he had to leave but that he wanted to link up again. I told him I was going back to P.R and he said he was coming out there soon.

I laid down in the room staring at the wall. I couldn't sleep so I got myself together and caught a cab to the airport. It was four in the morning and my phone was going off. I looked down and it was Hazel.

Hazel: *Hey. I know it's early, but I was having a weird dream about you. I wanted to make sure you were ok.*

Me: *I'm good. Just tired. Go back to sleep and call me in the morning.*

My plane left at 5:30 but I didn't get back until after nine. I was tired and just wanted to see my babies. I took the cab to Miguel's mom house and fortunately his car wasn't there. I knocked on the door and Karen opened it. She gave me

170

a hug and the kids came running to me. I knelt down hugging them and cried. I told Hazel I was back in town and she gave me the best news.

One of the houses I looked at was available, so she brought it and signed everything in my name. She had it furnished for the kids and me. The only thing I had to do was buy whatever sheets and comforters I wanted on the beds.

She picked us all up and we stopped by Target, Wal-Mart and Macys. When we got to the house, I found my personal stuff in one of the nightstands. I grabbed my checkbook and asked Hazel how much everything cost.

"I am not taking your money."

"What? Hazel please." She refused my money, but I would always have it just in case. I don't want anyone throwing shit back on me about what they did. I don't think she would, but I wasn't taking any chances.

That night, the kids and I ordered pizza and stayed up watching movies together. I allowed them to sleep in the bed with me since I missed them and didn't want to be away any longer.

Weeks went by since I came back, and Miguel and I haven't spoken or seen one another, and it was for the best. He would pick the kids up from his mom and drop them back off.

I was going to look at a place to open a small daycare like Heaven and Ang did back in the states. I was tired of sitting at home doing nothing. It was time for me to be independent like I used to be.

Miguel

The day Hazel brought me the letter back from Violet, I knew I had lost her forever. I'm not gonna lie, I was in my feelings and shed quite a bit of tears for her. It took me some time to get past the fact she wasn't coming back to me but fuck it; a new bitch will help you get over an old one.

I got rid of that bitch Pam and sent all the clothes she had to charity. I finally sold the house because it was nothing but bad memories and I'm staying in the one I've been staying at. The kids were comfortable here and it was like they never left.

I met some chick named Tammy who was a few years younger then me. She had a fat ass and her head game was on point. She was a bit clingy, but I didn't pay the shit no mind. When I had my kids, she knew not to call me because it was their time, no if, ands or buts about it.

She was aware of my ex wife who I signed the papers for and gave her the divorce she wanted. V and I went through my mom or sister about the kids and the drop off spot was at my moms.

As of right now she wasn't seeing anyone, but she was texting some dude back in the states. As long as he was over there, we wouldn't have a problem.

That's right I still kept tabs on her because no matter who I was with, she still had my heart and my kids.

I was on my way to drop them off at my moms when Hazel called to ask if I could take them home instead.

"Come on Hazel really."

"Yea ma is out. If you want, I can take them home."

"Nah, its fine. There's no need to keep them going in and out of cars in this rain." I hung up and drove to my ex-wife's house, parked behind Violets car and ran both the kids to the door. It was pouring like crazy out here.

I knocked on the door and Karen opened it. I didn't see V anywhere, and I was wondering where she was.

"Oh hey Miguel. Hey kids." She came out the room wearing just a robe barely covering her ass. Her hair was wet; I guess she just got out the shower.

"Hey." I said dryly trying not to get caught up in her looks. She was still beautiful as ever.

"Alright, I'll see you guys next week." I bent down to kiss the kids and Karen took them to the back to get ready for bed.

"Miguel." I heard her call as I was leaving.

"Yea V."

"Can you look at some paperwork for me real quick?"

"Yea where is it?" She pointed to the living room table. I glanced over it and noticed my name on some of it.

"You're opening a day care?"

"Yea. I just wanted you to know I put you down for emergency contact or if they needed any information, they can get it from you, if they can't reach me. Don't ask me what that's about. I don't recall Heaven and Ang doing that, but I am in a different country." She laughed. I missed the hell out of her goofy laugh.

"Why didn't you tell me? I would've had it done for you."

175

"It's ok Miguel. It's time I did stuff on my own. Besides we're not married anymore so you don't have to feel obligated to help me."

"Violet it doesn't matter we're not married. You're still my wife. Fuck that piece of paper." I felt myself getting angry.

"Boy cut it out. I see you with your new boo thing. She seems nice. Has she met the kids?" She asked walking upstairs.

"I'll be right back Miguel; let me put some clothes on." I know I should've left or waited but my heart would let me.

I made sure her front door was locked, shut the lights off and went up there to find her. I stepped in her room and she had a huge King-sized bed with satin sheets and comforter to match. I was pissed thinking about if she was about to let some nigga fuck her in here.

"No, she hasn't met the kids. What type of man do you think I am?" She jumped when she heard my voice.

"Miguel what are you doing in my room?" She pulled her tank top down over her breast.

"Oh you don't sleep in my shirts anymore?"

"What's wrong with you Miguel? And no, I don't because I don't have any to sleep in.

"Maybe if you asked for one, I would've gave it to you."

"Are you ok? I mean you're acting weird." I grabbed her by the waist and pulled her in front of me and looked in the mirror.

"You see this."

"Do I see what Miguel?"

"Us. This will always be." She moved outta my embrace and stared at me.

"Please don't do this to me. I can't take it Miguel." Her eyes started watering. I lifted her head with my finger and kissed her. She tried to fight me, but I wouldn't let her, and she finally gave in. She wrapped her arms around my neck and legs around my waist.

"Miguel stop, you have a girlfriend."

"She's not my girl. She's just a fuck." I told her taking my jeans off. She scooted back on the bed and gave me a bird's eye view of her wet pussy. I dove right in headfirst and had her screaming.

"I missed you V."

"I missed you too Miguel." I entered her slowly but forcefully. She seemed tighter then usual and it had me cumming fast again.

"Miguel, please tell me you didn't cum inside me."

"Why does it matter? No one else will ever have this pussy but me. I mean that shit. You even killed a nigga for trying." She froze. I guess she didn't think Mitch told me but that's ok.

"How did you know?"

"Never mind that; fuck me like only you can." And she did. It didn't matter how many women I slept with. I said it before, and I'll say it again. Violet hands down had the best pussy and would drain the hell out me every time.

"Miguel why do you keep cumming inside me?"

"Why do you keep allowing me to?"

"I'm trying to move but you're holding me down."

"Violet, you're having my babies. All ten of them." I noticed her look down at her wrist. I kissed the scars on both of them and then her stomach to let her know I felt her pain.

"I don't know Miguel. We're good right now." I wasn't trying to hear what she had to say. I leaned her over. had her touch her ankles and pounded harder inside until she couldn't take anymore. She tried to push me back but I was already letting my seeds go inside again. I guess she was over trying to stop me.

"I'm taking a shower are you coming?" She didn't have to ask me twice. We did things in there that should be illegal.

I was so drained after the shower; I fell straight to sleep. I woke up to V giving me head. Before I released myself, she turned her body, so we were in a 6'9 position. She and I fucked way into the morning. There was nothing off limits when it came to pleasing each other.

I woke up later and she was still lying on my chest drooling and all. It was a little after one and I didn't have shit to do, so I planned on staying here all day. Karen knocked on the bedroom door and I told her to come in. She smiled when she saw me still there. She told me a long time ago we would go through a lot of shit, but we were made for one another.

"Senor, the kids want to bring you two food. Is it ok to come in?" I nudged V to wake up as the kids came in behind Karen and she held the tray with the kids. They both hopped in the bed with us.

"Daddy, I want French fries Jr. said reaching on my plate for one. Joy was rubbing on Violet's face as she laid there watching us.

"Come here Joy." I said to her. I knew Violet couldn't sit up because she was naked under the covers. I turned both of their heads while she ran in the bathroom to get her robe. She got back in the bed and Joy helped me feed her some fries.

"Mmmm did you make these Joy?" She shook her head smiling.

"What did you do Jr.?"

"I watched. Daddy women cook right?"

"Yea son but sometimes men do too when they want to be nice to their wife."

"Are you going to cook for mommy?"

"I don't know. Mommy do you want me to cook for you?"

"Let me see. There's some things I want you to do for me but it's not in the kitchen." I laughed so hard I almost choked.

V and I stayed in the house all day with the kids. I turned my phone off but my burner phone stayed on no matter what. The only people who had that number were V and the people working for me.

I stayed the night again with V and we fucked most of the night. She and I were so tired that after the first few rounds, we both tapped out and went to sleep.

****

"Why are you so happy today Mickey? And who put those hickeys on your neck?" Hazel asked when she walked in my office.

"You nosy as hell."

"Well." She sat there with her arms folded.

"It was me." V said as she came in and sat on my lap. Hazel's mouth dropped to the floor.

181

"What?" V asked her.

"So are you guys back together?"

"No, but I'm fucking him, and I probably will continue until I find someone else."

"V, what I tell you about that shit?"

"Don't start Miguel. You have a fuck buddy. Bad enough, I allowed you to put another baby in me."

"Violet no you didn't."

"Girl, he wouldn't let me get up. He kept holding me there to make sure all his seeds made it in."

"I hate y'all, I swear." She laughed.

"Miguel, I just stopped by to bring you something to eat. I apologize for popping up. You know that's not my style."

"Violet, you don't ever need a reason to pop up on me."

"Bye Hazel." I said giving her a hint to leave.

"I'm telling you; you're having all my babies." I told her unbuttoning her pants and pulling her clothes off.

"Miguel just fuck me." I turned the Pandora up on my stereo surround, so no one would hear us. We had each other moaning over and over. V went to walk out and Tammy walked in.

"What the fuck are you doing here?" I yelled at her.

"What do you mean? We have lunch on Mondays and have been, for the last few weeks and who was that woman?"

"Ugh, you don't ever get to question me. But since you must know, that was my wife."

"Oh. Is everything ok? She didn't look upset."

"Why would she be upset?"

"You said y'all were going through a divorce."

"Don't worry about what we're going through. Let's cancel this Monday lunch thing. I'm not feeling it anymore."

She came closer and tried to sit on my lap. I stood up and walked her to the door.

"What's wrong. I thought we could have sex in here."

"Nah, I'm good. I'll call you when I get off."

"Ok, well have a good day." She went to kiss me and I turned my head.

"Oh, I see now. She must've tired you out huh?" She said pointing to the hickeys on my neck.

"Listen, I'm going to keep it 100 with you. Violet is my wife and will always be no matter what a piece of paper says. If she calls and wants me to make love to her, fuck her or even just to keep her company, I'm there. No woman will ever come before her or my kids so if you can't accept that, then I suggest you keep it moving. If you're wondering could I ever be faithful; no; not when my wife is where I really wanna be. Since she not fucking with me like that; I'll get what I can take from her and right now she wants my dick; so my dick is what she'll get. Do I make myself clear?"

"Crystal. Are you still coming over tonight?"

"I don't know but I'll call you when I'm gonna swing by." I couldn't believe after all that, she was still trying to fuck with me.

I had to see where V's head was at first. She was still in my sisters' office, so I went to check on her.

"You still here huh?" I asked leaning on the door.

"Yup. As long as I want that dick, you're going to give it to me? You are a mess and you didn't have to mean to her like that."

184

"What?"

"Bye Hazel, bye Miguel." Violet stood to leave.

"Am I stopping by tonight?" I pulled her close to me.

"Ugh, somebody is going to be waiting for you."

"Let her ass wait. You come before any bitch." I kissed her neck.

"Miguel, stop."

"I mean it."

"I'll see you later. Just do me a favor." She went to leave.

"Anything V."

"Don't fuck me right after you fuck someone else. And give me at least two days before you see me, if you do."

"Anything else?"

"Strap up my nigga." I couldn't do shit but laugh as she walked out the office.

Hazel

"I hope you know what you're doing?" I heard my sister say as I headed out her office.

"She and I had a talk before I left, and we decided; after we fucked for two days straight, we'll remain cool for the kids and when she needs it, I'll be here supplier."

"Miguel, you make it sound like you're a drug."

"I am. I'm her drug of choice." He was so stupid but I have to admit that he seems happier.

"You better not hurt her again or I'm shooting you myself."

"Damn, sis you would think you and I weren't blood and you two were. What are you gonna do if I find someone else?"

"I don't care who you deal with. No one will ever be my sister in law but V. I don't care if you had kids by another. I wouldn't claim them either."

"That's cold."

"No, that's how I feel. Violet is where you should be. I know that, you know that; hell everyone knows that."

"I know. One day, I'll get myself together and be the man she needs. Right now, I'm still stuck in my ways.

"What do you mean stuck in your ways?"

"I mean I wanna be with her and only her but every time I see a bitch with a fat ass or some big ass tities, my dick is ready to fuck her down. I don't know, maybe I have a sex addiction."

"You're fucking stupid." I told him.

"What? But seriously Violet has the best pussy ever. The sex between us is like no other and all these women can't compare or even begin to try and throw it on me like V."

"Ok, if V is all that, then why not just be with her? I mean you stalked the hell out of her, you won't allow another man to be with her so why don't you just step up and be the man she wants and needs?" He glared out the window he was standing next to and remained quiet. I leaned back in my chair watching to see if I could read him, but I couldn't.

"I will Hazel. I swear I will." He finally said and walked out. I know he was in love with V but like any other man, he always thought with his dick and until he could move past that, he would never be the man for her.

I stayed at work late to finish up some things when I heard the elevator chime and that bitch Faith walked off. She was shocked as hell to see me.

"What do you want?" I stood there with my arms folded. I thought I was bugging when I heard a shot and the bullet went past my head. I turned around and my brother was trying to kill her ass.

She took off down the steps and he brushed past me to follow her. I thought the shit was funny because never in a million years, did I think my brother would kill her. I guess when someone tries to take your life first the only thing left, is to return the favor.

I made sure everything was off and locked the office up. I took the elevator down because the steps and I did not get along. I always tripped down those damn things. When I got off, I was in the garage and Miguel was panting out of breath looking around.

"I take it she got away." I asked putting my stuff in the car.

"Yea, that stupid bitch is definitely gonna get what's coming to her." He said catching the keys to his truck I tossed at him.

"Where are you going now?" I asked with my window rolled down.

"I have to stop by mom's first, then I'm going home."

"A'ight."

"You know if you allowed Carlos and Joe to escort you to work they would've caught her dumb ass."

"Nah, I try to give them a break when I'm here. There's already so much security here."

"Yea well, be careful an I love you." I kissed his cheek and sat in my car.

"Love you too sis."

We both pulled out at the same time, in opposite directions. My security team was right behind me as I got to my house.

"Hey baby. I missed you today." I told my husband who was in the bed watching television.

"I missed you too. Come show me how much." He said rolling the covers back to show me he was naked underneath.

"Give me a few minutes to jump in the shower and then I'll give you what you need."

"Damn girl. Hurry up. I've been waiting all day for you." I took a quick shower and sure enough he was ready when I came out. I didn't even bother drying off as I crawled up the bed, stopping at his dick that was fully erect.

I took him in my mouth and he gripped on to the sheets right away. I had him releasing in minutes, but I wasn't finished. I stroked his dick back to life and slid down on top.

"Damn baby. Every time is like the first time with you. The way your pussy clings to my dick has me wanting to stay inside forever."

"Oh yea. How does it feel?"

"It feels real good Hazel. I love the hell out of you. Ride this dick."

"Shit Ricky, I'm about to cum." I came all over him.

We sexed each other for a few hours before I tapped out. I was exhausted from work and the shit with my brother. The only time I was at peace, was when I was home with my family. I was making it my business to start spending more time at home; shit I'm a boss I could work from here.

The next few weeks flew by and the guy from Brazil had us making even more money.

Miguel wanted to celebrate at the club and you know I'm always down for a party. Violet and Miguel were really only on their fuck buddy shit and dealt with one another when it came to the kids. Joy was turning one in a few weeks and I was helping her get things together for her party. She didn't have one for Jr. but she wanted to do it for Joy.

The night of the celebration, I wore some skintight high wasted denim jeans with a shirt that barely covered my breast. Violet had on a badass cat suit showing off all her curves. I knew my brother was going to pitch a fit when he saw her, but it didn't matter because he invited that chick Tammy and V was single.

She and I stepped into the packed club and all eyes were on us. My husband looked at me grinning. He was secure in his skin and he knew I was blessing him when we got home tonight. Miguel on the other hand had fire coming out of his ears and his eyes burned a hole in Violet as she stood at the bar laughing with some guy. I glanced back up at my brother and gave him the death, stare telling him he better not start no shit. The bitch Tammy was dancing in front of him; clearly oblivious to it all. I swear she was a dumb bitch; I mean who allows their man to continue fucking his ex and will drop everything to be with her. I don't know, maybe it's just me but I'm in no way allowing my man to do to me, what my brother doing to her.

Yes, V is still fucking him but she's not expecting anything in return. This other chick is trying to get where V is and I don't foresee it ever happening. He won't allow another chick to get close to him.

Violet and I stayed close to one another most of the night. All the men in there knew she was married to Miguel and kept their conversations with her clean and to a minimum. She grabbed me and told me to walk with her to the bathroom.

"Girl, the dude from Jersey I met is here." She said walking in.

"Ok so talk to him."

"FUCK! I don't feel like getting into anything with your brother."

"Oh, you won't because he's not thinking about you." We heard a voice in one of the stalls say. It was that girl Tammy he came with. She opened the stall and folded her arms.

"I don't think anyone was talking to you." I told her.

"I'm just saying. I'm getting tired of this game she has my man playing."

"She has your man playing? Honey, she isn't making him do anything he doesn't want to." Violet came out the stall to wash her hands, which this nasty bitch still, hasn't done.

"All I'm saying is, if she doesn't want him, then stop calling to get some dick." Violet started laughing and I knew it meant she was about to go in on her.

"Let's be clear about one thing Tammy. That man's dick belongs to me and always will. Yes, you get to go for a ride every now and then but when I call, he drops everything to ride the real ride. Now I don't have a problem with you because what y'all have going on has nothing to do with me. If you have a problem with it, then you should've never agreed to it when he kept it 100 with you at his office. I'm sorry to tell you this honey but he and I come as a package deal."

"A package deal?"

"Yes, a package deal. If you're fucking with him, then I will be there regardless so if you want to deal with him, then you'll have to deal with me being in his life too. And sometimes it means pulling him out your raggedy ass pussy and coming to where his real home is."

"If you are where is real home is, why isn't he there?" I shook my head because this bitch was about as dumb as they come.

"He's not there because I'm not ready to take him back yet. But when and if I do, be ready because you won't see him again."

"Whatever." She said rolling her eyes and walking out.

"You're not even going to wash your hands?" I yelled out behind her.

"Bitch, you crazy."

"No Hazel. I wasn't going to say anything but she had that shit coming. I think I'm about to end this fuck buddy shit with him too. He got this chick and that chick coming at me because he won't leave me alone."

"Well go out there and talk to your friend who came all this way to see you." I encouraged her to do her own thing because its clear my brother is.

"That's weird though isn't it? You think it's a coincidence he's here?"

"Ugh yeah. You said he had family. Maybe he's visiting and they brought him out."

"Yea I guess so."

We stepped out the bathroom and saw my brother and the chick arguing. He looked over at V smiling. He always got a kick out of how V put chicks in their place.

She and I stayed on the dance floor. She danced a few times with my brother and when she wasn't, her and the guy would converse at the bar. It was a good night minus the bullshit with Tammy.

Violet

The night of my ex's celebration party for his business was fun until his chick came to me on some other shit. I was ok with the arrangement he and I had, but I found myself wanting more and I know he wasn't ready for that.

I asked him to stop by today so I could tell him since the kids were home. It was better this way because I knew we would end up in bed together. He wasn't going to take it well because he knew, I could do as I pleased.

"Hey kids." I heard him say from the kitchen. Karen and I were getting the party bags and things together for Joy's party tomorrow.

We rented a hall due to who we were and no one needed to know our address. He wrapped his arms around my waist and kissed the back of my neck. The way he smelled and looked had my pussy soaked.

"Hey, can I talk to you real quick?" I asked taking him outside. I didn't want him yelling and if he was really mad, he could leave.

197

"What's up baby?" He kissed my lips and lifted my shirt to do the same with my stomach. He swore up and down I was pregnant, but I didn't have any signs and to be honest I didn't wanna know.

"Miguel, I think it's best if we stop whatever it is we're doing." He backed up and stared at me.

"Nah, that's not happening so you can cancel those thoughts right now."

"Miguel, this is not right. You're hurting that girl."

"Fuck that bitch. You think I care about hurting her? I told her from gate what it was and she agreed to it and so did you."

"You're absolutely right but now I'm finding myself falling back in love with you and you're still not ready. Honestly, I don't think you'll ever be ready to be with just one woman and I'm ok with it. I've done a lot of soul searching and I know my worth and this is me settling."

"V, I'm not trying to hear this shit. It's you and I forever. Fuck everybody else."

"That used to be us; now it's you and everyone else."

"This is because that nigga in town isn't it?" I was shocked but not really. I knew he would find out.

"This has nothing to do with him. Miguel if you told me right now you wanted to make it work and try again, I would never speak to him again. But I know you and you're not done doing you."

"Nah, this is because he's in town. You know he's a dead man walking right?"

"Stop it. I'm not bothering your chick and I've been respecting your relationship with her, why can't you do the same?"

"Because you're mine Violet. END OF FUCKING STORY!! I don't wanna talk about this shit anymore." He got in his car and pulled off.

I knew he would be mad but I had to let him know. I can't continue living like this. I went back in to finish helping Karen.

****

Today was Joy's party and as usual it was tons of people there from business associates to family. The party was in full swing with kids running around and old folks dancing and carrying on. Hazel came up to me with a disturbed look on her face it had me nervous.

"Violet, just remember this is Joy's party." I didn't now what she meant by it until I saw him and Tammy step in together.

"This motherfucker wants to play games I see."

"Hi Tammy, Miguel. Do you mind if I speak to him for a moment?" She had a smirk on her face. I guess she think she's won but I was going to have the last laugh.

"So this is the game we're playing?" I asked him and he thought the shit was funny.

"What? You said we were done. I didn't think it would be a problem bringing her here."

"Oh, you didn't think it would be a problem?" I laughed.

"Would it be a problem if I let that nigga come?" His entire facial expression changed.

"Don't play with me."

200

"Oh, it's not funny anymore huh? You brought your whore here trying to be funny but all you did was humiliate and embarrass the fuck out of me, out of your family." He didn't say anything.

"But it doesn't matter because you're this powerful man everyone bows down to so what they think don't mean shit."

"You're right it don't. We're not married and how am I embarrassing you or my family."

"These motherfuckers don't know we're divorced because you made sure to keep it quiet; yet you bring your whore up in here to your daughters party flaunting her in my face like it's nothing. You can be ok with that but I'm not."

"Violet." He tried to hug me and I pushed him away.

"I was supposed to be the strong wife who had your back no matter what, but this shit right here, shows me you really don't give a fuck about anyone but yourself. As long as you're not the one being embarrassed, fuck everybody else."

"V, I'm sorry. I didn't look at it like that."

"That's the problem. You never do. Now I have to go out here and play the happy wife who's ok with my husbands' mistress, when inside I'm dying. Our bond was supposed to be unbreakable in their eyes. How could you do this shit to me Miguel?" He tried to pull me in for a hug again.

"Don't touch me. I'm so over this shit. You want to play games, consider the game on."

"What the fuck is that supposed to mean?"

"Just what I said. Game on. Don't be mad when you see me in another niggas face." He tried to snatch my arm but I moved in enough time that he couldn't. I wiped my eyes and put on a brave face. I knew the Lord would help me get through this. I just prayed he could get me through the night because I was having those same suicidal thoughts as before.

Miguel stayed the entire party with her and I could see the faces of the other wives. They were just as disgusted with him as I was. No one was in denial about their men cheating but to flaunt the bitch around your family is something totally different.

A few of the wives came over giving me a hug; telling me they understood if I wanted to go outside and beat her ass or have one of them do it. I was shocked because I didn't speak to them a lot but to know they had my back made me look at them in a different light.

That night Miguel called me over and over. I kept sending him to voicemail before I made the decision to turn it off. He didn't have a key to this house, and I made sure I changed the code on the gate. I know he could bust through it but I was praying he would take the hint. I guess after a week, he got tired of trying because we went back to making the drop off spot at his mom's house.

Miguel had the kids for two more days and Jeremy text me to say he was still here and wanted to hook up. I had him pick me up a half hour away and we went to a restaurant in San Juan, which was about an hour away. I knew Miguel had a tracker on my phone and probably my car, so I left the phone in my car but had a burner one just in case he tried something stupid.

I only had security guys follow me when I was going anywhere besides his sisters or mom's and that's where I told them I was going. No one knew where I was and that was fine with me.

Jeremy and I ate by the water and had great conversation. I learned he had been stabbed by his ex because she walked in on him having sex with someone else. He told me he thought he was bisexual at one point in his life. But it turned out he was just trying it out. I was surprised he opened up to me about it but he explained it was something that happened.

He and his friend were drinking one night, and he woke up to the man giving him oral sex and he enjoyed it. As the story continued, he said the guy just wanted to be fucked and that's what he did but it was never done to him. They didn't carry on a relationship and it only happened a few times.

I gave him credit for giving me the option of deciding if I still wanted to be with him after he told me. Most men would just live a lie and expect you to stay when you found out.

We took a stroll outside hand in hand after we ate. I don't know what it was about him but he had me feeling some sort of way.

"Tell me a little more about yourself. Now that you know about me."

"Well, I have two kids who are the apple of my eye. My ex was the love of my life but couldn't keep his dick in his pants. His sister, mom and I are very close, and I don't have anyone occupying my time right now. I love kids; that's why I'm opening my own daycare and I love to shop."

"Hmmm, find me one woman who you know doesn't love to shop." He said making us both laugh. He turned my face to his and before I knew it, we were kissing each other hungrily out in the open. He pulled back and ran his hand down my face.

"I love the way you kiss; unfortunately, that kiss has me wanting more and I don't think either one of us is ready." He stood me up and adjusted his pants. I wanted him just as much as he wanted me.

"Let's get a room." I said snatching his hand.

We were downtown and hotels lined the streets. We stopped by the store on the way to pick up condoms. At the hotel, I went inside, rented it and led the way. My pussy was throbbing and I needed to feel him.

I threw him on the bed, stripped out of my clothes and stood there in my birthday suit.

"Damn you sexy as fuck." He whispered in my ear as he pulled me down on top of him. He had me climb on his face while he licked, slurped and sucked the shit out of my pussy.

"Shit, I'm cumming." I yelled out rolling off his face. He took his shirt off and used the back of his hand to wipe his mouth. He opened the box of condoms, put one on and plunged into me.

"Oh shit girl. This pussy good as hell." He was pounding into me bringing me to another orgasm. My legs started shaking and I released my juices on his stomach. He laid down on his back and asked me to ride him. I had that nigga speaking in tongues off my rodeo game. He came inside the condom and call me crazy, but I checked to make sure it didn't pop. He flushed it down the toilet and came back. I sat there playing with my pussy and he stroked himself to get hard again. He and I fucked a few more times before he tapped out. I kissed him goodbye and we both said we would stay in touch.

Ever since I broke it off with my baby daddy, I was horny. He may not be Miguel, but he was working with something and I needed it.

I laid in the bed crying for a while thinking about how my life was turned upside down by a dude who didn't give two shits about me and yet, I loved him to death.

My phone started buzzing and it was a text from Jeremy saying good night. I went to respond when there was banging at my hotel door. I opened it up and slammed it back; I was not in the fucking mood.

Miguel

I got home a little after nine from fucking Tammy.
Karen was at the house watching the kids because I still kept
the times with my kids just for us. My phone was going off but
I ignored it to check on my little ones. I gave them both a kiss,
shut the door and went in the living room to watch sports
center.

I must've fallen asleep because when I got up it was
after twelve. I turned everything off, used the bathroom and
went in my room to lie down. I looked at my phone and saw I
had twenty-four missed calls and a few picture messages.

To say I was heated, would be putting it mildly from
the way I was feeling when I saw those photos. There were
some of V with a dude at dinner, and them kissing on a bench
but the one that took the cake, is the one of her entering a hotel.

I didn't know who's number it was, nor did I care. I
zoomed in on the photo to see the name of the hotel and hauled
ass there. I knew exactly where it was being I've taken many
tricks there. I couldn't believe she used her own name to check

in; how dumb was she. I banged on that door until she opened it and slammed it back in my face.

"OPEN THIS FUCKING DOOR RIGHT NOW V." I was yelling in the hallway making people open their doors.

"Go away Miguel. I don't know what you're here for."

"If you don't open this door, I'm going to kick it down." It got quiet for a minute then I heard the lock click. She opened it and I flew passed her. There was no one in the room with her but by the looks of the bed, I knew someone was.

"You fucked that nigga." I was so mad, I had her by the hotel robe up against the wall.

"Does it fucking matter? You're fucking that bitch." She said smugly.

"V you just signed his death certificate and if I were you, I would head back to the states."

"I'm not going any fucking where. Get off me." I had the gun to her head.

"You think this is a fucking game V? Huh?" I knew I scared her. The tears were falling down her face.

"Really. You'll pun a gun on me after everything I been through?" I let her go and went in the bathroom to get some tissue. I felt bad for doing it but all that went out the window when I looked in the toilet and there was a condom floating. I lost it on her ass.

"I smacked her so hard, she flew across the room. She tried to get up and I kicked her in the stomach, back, face wherever I could. I felt strong arms pulling me away from her. Carlos and Joe had me against the wall.

"Yo boss, what the fuck? That's your wife, your kids' mother. Come on get yourself together." I looked over at V and she was laid out on the ground bleeding. Her face was swelling up and her eye looked like it was closed.

"Fuck that bitch. She wants to act like a ho, I'm going to treat her like one." I tried to go back and get her again, but they held me back.

"Yo Hazel, you need to get here quick. Your brother lost it and V needs to get to a hospital." I heard Carlos giving her the information on the phone.

As we were leaving, I felt a pain in my side, then another one in my leg. I turned around and Violet had the gun pointing at me before she shot me in the chest. I couldn't believe after everything she and I been through it's come to this.

"I hate you Miguel." Is the last I heard before everything went black.

Hazel

When Carlos called to tell me to get to some hotel an hour away to get V, I knew Miguel had to have found out about her date. I knew about it, but the room and fucking him was unforeseen. I was not expecting to see Violet looking like the elephant man or him being airlifted to an underground hospital.

My mom was going crazy because she loved V like her own daughter, but she didn't want to see her only son die either.

"What the fuck happened?" I asked V as we sat in the emergency department. Miguel was on his way to the underground doctor because once you get shot, cops get involved and no one had time for that.

"I'm officially done with him. I mean it from the bottom of my heart." She said crying and holding ice to her eye.

"Ok. I get that but tell me what happened." She told me how he came barging in the room and held a gun to her head. Then he went in the bathroom and just snapped. She didn't

212

know why at first until she went in and saw the condom floating in the toilet. My brother knew she slept with the dude but seeing the proof, drove him over the edge.

"V, what he did is unacceptable by all means and I would never, ever excuse this. All I'm asking is that you think about it when you say you're leaving. You know how much his kids mean to him and if you take them, I don't know what he'll do to you."

"Hazel, you can just hide me like before."

"V, the only reason I got away with it the first time was because he forgot about that house. If he remembered, he would've found you. There's no where to hide and is it fair to take his kids away from him?"

"Are you saying stay with him?"

"HELL NO! Violet, I would never tell you to stay with a man who almost killed you. I'm saying I think you two need to stay away from each other like you've been doing and keep the kids out of it. Those kids love their dad and you know that; they shouldn't have to suffer because it didn't work out between the two of you."

"Mrs. Rodriguez." The doctor came in the room to give her the test results back.

"Yes."

"You have a few bruised ribs but that's nothing we're too concerned about but what does have me concerned, is the fact you didn't tell us you were three months pregnant." Both of our mouths dropped open and she started crying harder.

"Oh, I'm sorry. I didn't know she wasn't aware. I'm going to give you some pain pills that don't have narcotics in them and won't affect the baby. I'm also prescribing you some prenatal pills as well. I want you to follow up with a GYN quickly to keep and eye on the baby."

Once she was discharged, I brought her to my moms' house and left her to go check on my brother. I got there and Carlos explained to me what happened and what he walked in on.

"So, you're telling me he was beating on her like she was a dude and called her a ho?" He shook his head yes and I looked at my mom who was crying her eyes out but I didn't know for who.

The doctor came out a little while later and told us he was fine. He was shot three times but nothing life threatening. He was wearing a vest so the bullet in his chest didn't do anything, but he lost a lot of blood from the shot in his leg and side.

"How did he get hit in the side if he had on a vest?" I questioned because it didn't sound right.

"I guess the shooter didn't have a good aim because she got him directly under it." He said opening the door so we could go in.

"I'm fine. I'll see you later?" This nigga was sitting up on his phone.

"Can you bring Tammy here? She's worried about a nigga." He said laughing thinking the shit was cute.

"HELL FUCKING NO!" He sucked his teeth and looked at my mom.

"What are you crying for? I'm fine."

"I'm not about to give you a long speech." I said.

"Good, cause I don't want to hear it. The bitch shot me three times, but she should've killed me because now I'm

215

going to kill her and that nigga she fucked." He hopped off the table and almost fell.

My brother was showing the side he only showed when dealing with people who did him wrong, snitches or even people he just didn't like. But he was on a mission now to kill her like he wasn't wrong.

"Shut up. You're not killing her." He stood face to face with me. Well, I'm shorter then him but you know what I mean.

"Where is she?"

"Tuh, like I would tell you."

"She can't hide forever sis. Remember that. I may be hurt now but I will find her and when I do, its lights out." He shouted walking out slowly with Carlos and Joe who were shaking their heads.

I snatched my mom up and raced back to her house hoping he didn't go there. I pulled up and he wasn't but I knew he was coming if not tonight, tomorrow or the next day but he was coming.

"V are you ok." My mom asked her. When she looked up from the bed my mom gasped and then started screaming

216

when she saw her face. I guess the flashbacks of what my father did came back to her. She rocked V in her arms like a kid and tried to stop herself from crying.

"V, I'm so sorry this happened to you. I don't know what's wrong with my son." Just as she said it, there was banging at the front door. We knew it was Miguel and had to hide V quick. My mom told her to hide in the closet in her room since he never goes in there. I laid on the couch and had my mom answer the door.

"I know you heard me knocking Hazel."

"And your ass has a key. Why would I answer the door for a woman beater anyway?" I sat up.

"You know you talked all that shit about daddy beating on mom and even took his life for it, and you turned out to be the same fuck nigga as him." I knew I pissed him off because he got up and went in the kitchen with my mom.

"Where's V?" Carlos whispered.

"She's safe for now."

"Well he's on a rampage looking for her. This nigga put a $250,000 bounty on her head."

"He did what?" My phone started ringing and it was Ricardo asking me what happened and why was there a bounty out on V. I told him I'd call him back.

"Really fuck nigga?" I mushed him upside the head.

"Hazel, keep your hands off me."

"Since you want to sit in here and play the innocent roll like you didn't do shit to make her shoot you, tell mommy how you just put a $250,000 bounty on Violet's head. Go ahead nigga tell her."

"Miguel, you didn't."

"Ma, she needs to pay for trying to kill me."

"And who's going to make you pay for what you did to her? Huh?" I had my arms folded.

"She should've taken that ass whooping like the BOSS BITCH she is. We would've gotten past it but no, she tried to kill me."

"I would've done the same thing."

"Ma, I'll see you tomorrow because I can see I'm not getting anywhere with her here."

"Why don't you just whoop my ass to shut me up? Huh?" I got in his face. He laughed and stood up.

"Because you're my sister."

"And she was your wife. The mother of your kids. Miguel, you beat her like she was a man on the streets, like you never gave two fucks about her. And you thought I was going to bring the bitch Tammy to see you. She's the reason all this shit started."

"Go head Hazel."

"No, you want the truth. I'm going to give it to you. Violet worshipped the ground you walked on from the first time you told her you loved her. She did any and everything to please you and it wasn't good enough. You cheated on her multiple times and she took you back because she loved you. She almost killed her self over you but instead lost a child, all because you couldn't keep you dick in your pants. Then, she lets you back in her heart again, only to be told you would still continue to fuck others but she can't. Last but not least, she finally found someone to occupy her time and move on with her life and you get all up in your feeling because she gave him

219

the pussy." I knew I was pissing him off by the way he was

balling up his fist.

"Ok Hazel, that's enough." My mom said grabbing my

arm.

"No ma he needs to hear this shit. Maybe it'll do his

dumb ass some good. All she ever tried to do was love you and

all you did was step on her and treat her like shit. That woman

didn't want your money, cars, houses, nothing; just your heart

and love. Was it that hard for you to give it to her?" He didn't

say anything.

"Now you have a woman who was your wife, your so

called everything, looking like a gang of bitches beat her with a

pipe and ready to skip town with the kids all because Miguel

couldn't take her moving on. Well guess what? She gave you a

million chances and you blew every one of them. Now you

walking around here with a bounty on her head and trying to

kill her. You are fucking pathetic. I hate you so much right

now that I can't stand to be in your sight." I shoulder checked

him and walked out the kitchen. I had Carlos and Joe go in the

kitchen to keep him occupied while I got V out of my moms'

room. She ran to the car with me, jumped in the back seat and hit the floor.

Ricardo opened the door when I got there and helped me bring her in. I ran her a bath and closed the door.

"Yo, Miguel did that shit to her?" I shook my head yes and told him everything that happened. He wanted to go over there but then he would know V was at the house, so I asked him not to see him until tomorrow. He probably figured Ricardo was sleep and I would tell him in the morning.

"Baby, I'm going to let her stay her with us. She wants to stay in the basement; there's a living room, bathroom and a huge bedroom down there. She said it'll be like her own place except for the kitchen. Once he calms down and takes the bounty off her head, I'll take her home but until then I don't feel safe with her anywhere else."

"You know I don't mind. But what about her kids?"

"They can stay with my brother and I'll get them whenever she wants to see them. Somehow, we'll have to explain to Jr. he can't say he saw her. Joy isn't really talking as much yet so we should be good."

"Ok baby. I love you. I'll go talk to him tomorrow." I jumped in the shower after I got V settled, had her turn her phone off so he couldn't track her and gave her one of the burner phones we always had. It was the newest galaxy, but no one had the number but me. I gave her a hug and went upstairs to go to sleep. I had enough of my own shit to deal with and now my brother was on some Rambo type shit with his baby mother. I can't wait to see what happens tomorrow.

Violet

I couldn't believe this is where Miguel and I are at in this point of our lives. Two kids, a failed marriage and a battered woman is not where I saw myself. If someone would've told me three years ago this would be me, I would smack them silly.

The fact still remained after all this; I was still in love with him. Don't get it twisted now, I wasn't taking him back. Yes, he beat on me this one time and because I shot him, doesn't mean my love goes away. I'm sure it's going to take time to get over one another but it sure is going to be a bitch doing it.

I was happy to have Hazel in my life as my best friend. Even though he was her brother, she didn't care about having my back. She let his ass have it at their mom's house and I couldn't have said it any better. See men will only do what we women allow but the minute you give it back to them, they can't take it.

I'm not going to lie, when he showed up at the hotel room I was scared to death. I didn't think he would get that mad about me sharing my pussy; shit he sharing his dick. At least I was protecting myself, who knows what his ass was doing. Now I'm staying with his sister, I'm three months pregnant which is my fault too and I don't know when I'll be able to see my kids.

My life really sucks but I'm trying to stay strong and keep those thoughts from creeping back in my head. That was selfish of me to try and take my life and I guess the Lord taught me a lesson because he took my child.

I could hear yelling upstairs as I sat at the bottom of the steps listening; it was Miguel and Hazel going back and forth again about the shit he did and how she still wouldn't be able to hide me forever. *Fuck, how did he know she was hiding me?*

"Nigga, aint nobody hiding her. Maybe she finally figured a way to keep you off her scent."

"Whatever, Hazel. When you talk to her, you tell her if she wants to see the kids before she dies, she will have to go through me."

"You still trying to kill her I see."

"Why not? She tried to kill me."

"How are you going to explain to your kids that their mom was taken by their controlling ass father who was mad their mom fucked someone else?"

"You know what Hazel; I see you really have more love for her then you do me. If I didn't know any better, I would say you know where she is."

"Miguel, you are my brother and I love you with all my heart but what you did to her was wrong, so yes I'm going to take her side. Should she have shot you? No. But what did you expect her to do when you almost killed her? You said yourself when Otis had his hands all over her and kissing on her, she handled herself well dealing with the situation. She could've killed you but she didn't. Violet aint no dummy, and her murder game is on point. So you can sit here and talk all the shit you want, but you know as well as I do, if she wanted you dead at that moment when she pointed the gun at you, she could've done it." He must've been trying to process what she said because he was quiet for a while. I thought he left until I heard him speak again.

"Well then she should've done it because then I wouldn't be dying inside right now thinking about another man touching her or giving her pleasure. That shit is fucked up Hazel on so many levels." I felt the tears coming out my eyes, but I stayed strong and sat there.

"How do you think she felt when those women told her they've been sleeping with you? Huh? Don't you think she was dying inside too? She only slept with this guy one night and you slept with these women multiple times and still took your ass home to her. She never raised her hand to fight you nor did she try to kill you but look what you did. Violet is a tough ass chick and she really has some thick skin when it comes to loving you."

"I love the fuck out of her and this shit got me going crazy." I heard him say. I was so weak for this man. I went to turn the doorknob, but he left before I was able to see him and maybe it was for the better.

"Hey. Sorry you had to hear us arguing." I went into the kitchen to grab something to eat.

It had been two weeks since the shit went down and this was the first time he came to her house. I was surprised he poured his feelings out to her but they were tight like that.

My face finally cleared up all the way. Today is my first prenatal appointment and Hazel was getting the kids. I missed them.

"Hazel, I appreciate everything you've done for me AGAIN." I stressed.

"But I need to go home now. My face cleared up, I miss my babies, my bed and my house. If he wants to kill me then so be it. I can't keep running like this from him."

"I understand. He went to work so that'll give us some time to run some errands before I take you home." She said.

The doctor said the baby's heart rate was great and I should expect a healthy baby despite the horrible mugging I endured. Yea, had to go with that.

We stopped by the store and I loaded up on at least a month's worth of food, snacks, juices and some other crap. I would send Karen out for milk, bread and eggs if I needed it.

I had just finished putting the last bag in the trunk and Hazel was taking the cart back to the drop off section, when I felt a gun on the back of my head.

"Well, well, well if it isn't the bitch who has a bounty on her head." I heard some man say. I didn't know who he was nor did I care.

"Put the fucking gun down before I blow, you're head off in this parking lot?" Hazel yelled out with her berretta aiming at him. He dropped it and put his hands behind his head. She stepped in front of him and you would think he saw a ghost.

"Oh shit. I'm sorry Ms. Rodriguez. I didn't know she was with you. There is a bounty on her head and I was just trying to collect. Please don't kill me. I need to feed my family." He was begging and pleading for his life.

"Here's $1000. Don't mention this shit to anyone and we won't have a problem."

"$1000 dollars. The bounty was for $250,000." She shot him straight in the forehead without a second thought. Luckily, we were at the far end of the lot and no one was watching. She made a call and had someone there in minutes cleaning him up. These two siblings really were the boss. She sent someone in with the money she offered the guy and got the surveillance from the lot.

We parked in front of my house, took the bags inside and put the groceries away. She told me she would be back later to drop the kids off because she was going to stop by the office and do a little work.

I straightened the house up and went upstairs to take a nice hot bath. I threw in some bath tablets from Bath & Body Works, turned on Pandora to the Sade station. It was something about her voice that soothed me.

I stepped inside the tub and laid there. Before I knew it, I had tears cascading down my face and I had no idea why. I tried to wipe them, but I had suds on my hands. I went to reach for a towel when someone passed me one. I jumped and once all the soap was out my eyes, I came face to face with the person I thought never wanted to see again.

Miguel

I sat outside Violet's house watching her and my sister bring groceries in the house. I knew where she was the entire time because Ricardo told me.

The day after all the shit happened, he came over and we got into it so bad we almost came to blows. I know he was like a brother to V so when he saw her, it probably fucked him up.

I had to wait two weeks before I could go see her but when I got there today, I just couldn't. My mind was still fucked up. My sisters' security told me she had to body a guy who tried to collect on the bounty I had out on Violet, which I forgot to stop.

I watched Hazel give her a hug and then rub V's stomach and smiled. I knew in my heart; I had knocked her up again. She must've just found out because after last time, I knew she wouldn't hold it in again.

I waited for my sister to leave and sat there for over two hours debating if I should go in. I locked the door behind me and went to where I heard the music coming from. I leaned on the door watching her cry. My heart was hurting, and I was in pain just like she was. She tried to wipe her face, but the soap stopped her. I handed her the towel and I saw nothing but fear on her face.

"If you're here to kill me, take me somewhere else so my kids don't find me?" She said stepping out the tub. I followed her in the room, and she did her regular routine as far as drying off, putting on lotion and getting in the bed.

"Don't get under the covers." She looked at me like she was confused. I stepped closer, lifted the shirt back up and leaned down to kiss her stomach. I heard her sniffling and wiped the tears with my thumbs.

"When did you find out?" I sat on the bed and let her sit on my lap.

"The day I went to the hospital." She said still sniffling. She got up and went to the bathroom to get tissues. She was still beautiful with a puffy red nose and all.

"How far are you?" She sat on the bed, instead of my lap and pulled her legs to her chest.

"Three and a half now." I smiled. There wasn't a doubt the baby was mine because I saw the condom but just knowing I did her like that and she was; is killing me.

I laid back on the bed and blew my breath. I wasn't used to this apologizing shit, but I knew in my heart it had to be done. If she didn't accept it, that's on her.

"I'm sorry." We both said at the same time. I sat up.

"V, you don't have anything to be sorry for. What I did to you was foul and you deserved to protect yourself. I was in my feelings and I never took the time out to see how bad I was hurting you. I took you and your love for granted; I played with your heart and emotions. I never thought you would find someone else and give him your body."

"Miguel." I stopped her from speaking.

"I was so busy giving everyone else what they wanted, I never thought about giving you what you needed and that was me. All these bitches wanted me for my money, houses and other shit and all you wanted was me. Violet, I was blinded by my past and all the abuse I went through, that I did it to you." I took her hand in mine.

233

"I apologize to you from the bottom of my heart V. I never wanted to hurt you and I did. I love you so much and when I found out you slept with him, I snapped. I didn't even see you as the person I was hitting. I saw my father and I was beating on him, the way he used to beat my mom. You don't have to forgive me but I needed to say it because it was weighing heavy on me." She was crying hysterical and didn't know why.

"Miguel, I love you so much. it hurts. I know you snapped and I'm sorry for giving my body away before we were really officially over. I needed some time and attention from you, and he gave it to me."

"What you mean?" I asked.

"He listened when I talked, he enjoyed my company, and he sent me texts throughout the day just to say he was thinking about me. All the things you used to do; you stopped to do for someone else and then another and another; never once taking care of me. Somewhere along the line you got lost and I can't tell you where. Miguel when we're together, we're so good but when you're off its bad. This is the worst I've seen, and I can say, I never want to relive that day." I stood up and pulled her to me for a hug.

"That shit will never happen again. I promise on my kids I will never put my hands on you again."

"I needed that apology Miguel. I feel like you really meant it."

"I did V. I would never intentionally hurt you." She stood on her tippy toes and pecked my lips a few times before sticking her tongue inside. I was taken aback by it at first, but I didn't stop her either. She took her shirt off and placed my hands on her chest. A nigga aint going to lie, she had my dick all the way hard.

"V, I don't think we should do this." She unbuckled my jeans and pulled my boxers down.

"Why? Do you have a girlfriend?"

"No, but..." My conversation was cut short when she swallowed me whole. I put my head back and she wet my dick up and brought me to a much-needed release. After the shit happened with us, I cut all my side chicks off. Tammy was still clingy as hell, but I was going to change my number tomorrow anyway.

"Mmmm you still the taste good Papi." She sucked everything out like a vacuum.

I lifted her up and pushed her back on the bed. I got on my knees and let her make it rain in my mouth so many times she pushed me off. It was time for me to fuck her and mentally, I didn't know if I could. She had let someone else touch her and I was definitely in my feelings.

"We don't have to Miguel. It's ok." It was like she read my mind. I couldn't go out like that though. I placed the tip at the opening and she grinded on it. I kissed her aggressively to try and take my mind off. I felt her grab my dick and force me inside her.

"Shittttt V." She was still tight, and her pussy still curved to my dick.

"Miguel, this is your pussy and yours only. I know it was hard for you but now that you're in, I need you to make love to me." I heard the sincerity in her voice. She wanted and needed me, and I felt the same towards her. I gave her the slow strokes she loved.

"V, I love you. Do you think we could try one more time?" I asked waiting for her response.

"The minute you entered me, I was your woman again. I love you too baby." I felt tears coming from my own eyes this time. She kissed each one away and at that very moment, I was going out of my way to be the best man for her. My playing days were over, this is where I needed to be.

"Don't leave me V. It's going to take some time to get used to being a one woman man but work with me."

"Miguel, I'm about to cummmm." She yelled out scratching my back.

"Me too baby. Fuckkkkkk." I let so many seeds out, I'm sure she would've got pregnant again. I rolled off and she took her hand to stroke my man back to life again.

"V, you have to give me a minute."

"Never. My man never taps out before me."

"Oh, I didn't tap out. I just need a few minutes."

"No you don't look. Your wife has the miracle hands."
We both laughed as she climbed on top and rode us both to a climax. She grabbed my hand to take a shower with her and you know it we had sex in there too. We could go all night if you let us; that's just how we were.

She put on one of my wife beaters with some of my boxers I had there. She went downstairs to make something for us to eat but it was getting late, so I told her to order pizza. I already called Karen and told her to bring the kids to the house.

"V are you gonna be my wife again?" I asked her. She was lying on top of me on the couch.

"Do you want me to be?" She looked up at me.

"I never wanted you to divorce me."

"I would love to be your wife again but on one condition."

"What's that?"

"We have to go to at least two marriage counseling sessions, and you need to see an anger management specialist. I'm not saying you have to sit in meetings with anger management, I just think maybe you can talk to someone about controlling your anger that's all. If you can do that for me, I'll be your wife again."

"Done." I sent my secretary a message telling him to find the best marriage counselor and anger management specialist and call them to set up an appointment.

"What are you doing?" She asked me to laugh. I showed her the text.

"Baby, you could've done that Monday morning."

"Nope. I meant what I said. I will do anything to have you back and the faster I get this done, the better. I love you woman."

"I love you too man. Let me show you how much." She went and spoke into the microphone again and I enjoyed every minute of it. She and I ended up sexing each other again before the kids got to the house.

"You know your dream house is sitting there empty."

"I know. I would love to look at it now that it's finished before you sell it."

"Baby, I would never sell it. That's yours and you can move in whenever you want."

"Yea but Hazel brought this house for us."

"No she didn't. She rented it. She knew damn well I was letting you move in your dream house. That's why she didn't take your money when you offered to pay for it."

"Oh you wait until I see her." She and I laughed and played around with one another until Karen walked in with the kids. They were so excited to see their mom and she was too.

The next day V and I took the kids out to the park; then ice cream. She and I were in the mall with the kids when Tammy came up to me talking shit.

"You're back with this bitch, that's why you can't answer my phone calls."

"Tammy, go ahead before I have you thrown the fuck out."

"Daddy who's that?" Now see, this the type of shit I didn't like. No jump off ever approached me when I was with my family. They knew the rules but this right here just signed her death certificate.

"Come on Jr. Let's go over here while daddy talks to his friend." That's why she was my wife. She already knew what time it was with this bitch and gave me my moment to get rid of her.

"What the fuck is wrong with you? You know better." I asked her. She stood there looking dumb as hell.

"I'm pregnant." I laughed so hard that other people started looking.

"Yea right bitch. There has never been a time when I didn't strap up. And if I thought the condom broke, you know dam well I had you get up. Try something else."

"Well I could've been if you weren't far up her ass. Why didn't you want a baby with me?" She started crying and I thought I was being punked.

"Are you serious right now?"

"Yes. Miguel, I'm in love with you and I know you love me too."

"Ok, you're bugging. The only woman I love and will ever love, is over in that store with my kids. My heart belongs to her and her only."

"Well I happen to know she fucked somebody else in a hotel a few weeks back."

"Ok and. She and I were on a break and why are you checking for her anyway. She is not your concern. Listen, I'm sorry if you're in love with me but I'm not the one for you. Now if you'll excuse me."

"Yo boss look out." This bitch pulled a gun out on me and within seconds her brain was spread all over the mall. People were running while we stood there waiting for a clean up crew. Carlos went to the security section to get the footage and we were home not too long after.

"That is why your ass needs to be with one woman." She wrapped her hands around my waist and kissed me.

"Yup, and that's why you're the one I chose."

Hazel

"So you killing bitches at the mall now?" I asked my brother when he walked in my house.

"Whatever. That crazy bitch pulled a gun out on me."

"That'll teach you about slinging dick, now won't it."

"Shut up. Listen, V is giving me one more chance and I don't wanna fuck it up this time."

"I already know."

"I know, you know smart ass. I'm saying, I want you to bring her down to the courthouse for me later so we can get remarried."

"Damn, I didn't know she was doing that. You two must've fucked and made up."

"Shut yo ass up. Are you going to do it or not?"

"Yea as long as she wants to marry you. Don't have me get her down there and she be like hell no."

"You know I can't stand you right?" He said closing the door.

"What time jerkoff?" I yelled behind him as he got in the car.

"3:00. Afterwards we're gonna celebrate at the club."

"It's early as hell to go to a club."

"Who cares? Its for my wife. She can't drink but she loves to party."

"You're crazy."

I called my mom to inform her he was getting married, but he stopped there first. She was already trying to find something to wear.

V was at the beauty salon getting her hair and nails done so I just stayed home with my man and daughter watching movies. We got to the courthouse a little before 3 and found a seat in the office. It was tight inside, but it was only a few of us.

V got there dressed in a fitted white dress that came just above her knee and showed off her small stomach. She wore the same veil she did in her first wedding and her shoes were Jimmy Choos. My sister in law always had style.

Miguel got them new wedding bands for a new wedding. Violet said her vows to my brother, and he teared up a little. He said his and V cried, making everyone else cry. These two were made for each other; I was just happy they figured it out.

We got to the club after 6 because we went out to eat and dropped the kids off. All of V's family came back up from Jersey. They didn't care. It was always a reason for them to vacation and party. We stayed at the club all night and Violet and my brother molested each other on the dance floor most of the night.

The next day I got a package delivered to my house, which was unusual because I never gave my address out. Even my mail went to a PO box. I opened the big brown envelope and it was a letter addressed to V. I called my brother because her phone was off. He didn't answer because he was walking through the door.

"What's up sis?" He asked going to the safe to get something. I followed behind him.

"Mickey somebody sent this to V." He looked at me, then took the envelope.

"Who is it from?"

"I have no idea. Whoever sent it must not have known where she lived. But how did they get my address?"

"I'll open it."

"Mickey, that's to V."

"Yea and V is my wife." He shrugged his shoulders and opened it.

"What the fuck? I knew this shit was going to come back." He dropped the letter and took off out the house. Yup, my nosy ass picked it up to read it.

Dear Violet,

I had a great time with you. Every conversation, every date and the sex, well that was an added bonus. I loved the way you had me saying your name. It's sad to say, you and your fuck boy husband are going to suffer a terrible loss. If I don't have 100 million dollars in this account by tonight, bodies are going to start dropping. Oh, don't think I don't

know your man has it.

    See you soon.

    I looked at the date of the letter and it was dated for yesterday. I picked my daughter up and called my husband first, then my mom. I wanted all of us to meet at my brothers' house to figure out who this was. All three of us pulled up at the same time along with a shit load of bodyguards. I could hear my brother in the house yelling at the top of his lungs.

    "What's wrong?" I saw my niece and nephew sitting on the couch staring at my brother.

    "She's gone."

    "Who's gone?" I sat my daughter on the couch next to them.

    "Violet man. They took her a few minutes before I got here." He said throwing another note on the ground.

    Y'all thought I was playing. Now I have to show you what I mean. This bitch is my collateral. If I don't get the money, I'm sending her home piece by piece. And don't think I didn't notice she's pregnant. Mmmmm, that pussy is going to

feel real good before I kill her.

Violet

I never expected Miguel to show up at my house that night and pour his heart out to me. Yes, he was he love of my life, but I knew he wanted me dead too. The look in his eyes and the anger and hate he had towards me, didn't make me think he'd change his mind.

I probably should've made him wait longer before I took him back but I needed him. People can say what they want but when you're in love with someone, we do things others may not agree to but it's not up to them to agree. I'm the only one who has to wake up with that man everyday and if I choose to be with him then, it's all that matters.

I was happy he agreed to marriage counseling and anger management classes. I wanted us to start fresh and work together to keep our bond tight without any of these heffas trying to get in the middle of what we have.

Yesterday, I remarried the man of my dreams in front of a small room full of people. When he said he wanted to say his own vows, I figured they would be the same as our first wedding. The words he spoke had me hysterical crying.

Violet, you are everything a man can want in a woman and the fact you chose me, makes me feel like I won the lottery. You came into my life and held me down even when I know you should've walked away.

The pain I instilled on your heart and in your mind was enough to leave and never come back but not you; you were determined to get me to give you all of me. I'm here right now like the shadow on your side telling you that I'm giving you all of me.

My heart, mind, body, soul and anything else you need from me. I know you have questions on your mind if I'm going to treat you the same, but you can be sure, as the sun is yellow, I won't. I know my heart. From now on, I only want you crying happy tears and I'm sure I'll make mistakes trying to get it right for you but I'll never break your heart again. You'll never have to question my love because you are the only one that has ever had it. For better or worse, I'll love you with ever beat of

my heart. I love you Violet Rodriguez.

I keep replaying those words in my head as I sit here in this dark ass room. I remember playing with the kids and there being a knock at the door. I went to answer it, and someone wearing a ski mask put something over my nose. I should've asked who it was at first, but no one knew where we lived, or so I thought. Shit; my kids. I hope they're ok. I wonder if anyone knew I was missing yet?

I know my husband is going to lose it when he finds out? I had so many thoughts running through my head, I barely noticed someone else sitting across from me grinning.

"What are you doing here?" The person smiled, walked over and landed a huge slap on my face. That shit stung like hell. I thought about getting up to fight the person because I wasn't tied up but I had to think of my baby.

"You don't get to ask any questions."

"See your man is going to pay us what we're owed. And then we may release you but until then, you'll be right here." The person walked around my chair sniffing me.

"Yo, back the fuck up from her." The person acted like they were frightened by him.

"Why do you care if I'm around her?"

"Just back the fuck up. We trying to get this money and I can tell you right now if the nigga thinks for one second someone laid a hand on her, we can forget about collecting shit."

"How much did you ask for?"

"$100 million. I would say that's enough for her. Don't you think? He should be broke after that." He asked the person and grabbed their hair. They were so stupid; my husband would've given up his entire bank account for me.

"Bend that ass over while I tie her up." He didn't do it too tight but enough that I couldn't get out of it.

"Do you have a condom?"

"Yea right. I ain't never used one before." I was disgusted they were getting ready to fuck in front of me.

"Can you fuck somewhere else?" It slipped out my mouth and I regretted saying it as soon as it left my lips.

"Oh, you too good to watch. Matter of fact, I'm going to give you front row seats." I didn't know what he meant by that until he untied me and pushed me on the couch.

"Please don't do this." I said out as they started trying taking my clothes off. I refused to go down without a fight. Miguel and I could have more kids. I punched one of them in the face and kicked the other one in the balls. I was beating the brakes off the person until he grabbed me by my hair and slammed me back on the couch and hit me so hard, I passed out.

I woke up I guess a few minutes later with him pumping in and out of me. The other one was sucking on my chest and rubbing on my clit. I think they were trying to make me cum. I tried to push them off me but it just wasn't working.

"Miguel, where are you?" I screamed out.

"He won't find you."

"Oh, he's going to find me and when he does, I'm going to make sure he tortures both of you before he kills you."

"Shut the fuck up." The one sucking my chest said.

"Shit, this pregnant pussy is good as hell. That's my first time every fucking someone pregnant." He said still pumping in and out.

BOOM!!! I heard a loud noise coming from the top of the house. I heard my baby's voice, but I couldn't see him.

"MIGUEL." I shouted.

"Violet where are you?"

"Baby, I'm right here."

"Let's get the fuck out of here." They threw their clothes back on and had me stand up but my body fell back down.

"Hurry up. I heard another voice coming from a door in the wall.

"What the fuck did yall do to her? Miguel is going to murder everything moving when he sees her like this. Shit, yall fucked up bad. Let's go." I knew the voice and if I made it out of here, I was going to kill her. I heard footsteps coming down the stairs and I pointed to the door they ran out of.

"Baby, I'm here. Are you ok?"

"They raped me." I saw the look on Miguel's face, and I knew they were all going to be sleeping with the fishes soon.

"How many were there?"

"It was two but then another one came right before you got down the steps."

"I got you V."

"I knew you were coming for me."

"You damn right. I love you." He said and carried me out the house. There was an ambulance waiting for me. He jumped in the back with me.

I woke up in the hospital and he was sitting there talking to his mom, Carlos and Joe.

"Hey baby." He rushed to my side.

"How are you feeling V?"

"I'm ok. Is the baby ok?"

"Yes, he is ok." He told me smiling.

"So it's a boy huh?"

"Yea. They checked you for everything. Baby, I need to ask you a question and I don't want you to be ashamed because it wasn't your fault."

"No, he didn't cum in me. You got there just in time." I saw the relief wash over his face.

"The doctor gave you an antibiotic and a shot of penicillin just to be sure."

"V, I have one more question."

"It was Faith, Pam and the guy I couldn't catch his voice because he kept his face covered with some mask. He disguised his voice."

"Faith and Pam."

"Pam was raping me with the guy. Faith came to get them when you were upstairs and told them they fucked up. It was three of them baby." I said crying. He got in the bed with me and held me close.

"All Faith's family is dead. I want her found yesterday. I want everybody in Pam's family dead and on CNN by the morning. I don't give a fuck if she has a relative giving birth. I want them dead and the bastard she delivered. If there's a baby daddy, I want him and his family dead too. I want them to know they fucked with the wrong motherfucker. I want the world to know that you don't come for me or my family without repercussions. Niggas want to come for my wife; I'm killing their whole family tree and any seeds planted."

TO BE CONTINUED......

Made in the USA
Middletown, DE
04 February 2021